THE
YOUNG FORESTER

THE
YOUNG FORESTER

ZANE GREY

G.K. Hall & Co. • **Chivers Press**
Thorndike, Maine USA   **Bath, England**

This Large Print edition is published by G.K. Hall & Co., USA and by Chivers Press, England.

Published in 1998 in the U.S. by arrangement with Golden West Literary Agency.

Published in 1998 in the U.K. by arrangement with Golden West Literary Agency.

U.S. Softcover   0-7838-0295-1   (Paperback Series Edition)
U.K. Hardcover   0-7540-3491-7   (Chivers Large Print)
U.K. Softcover   0-7540-3492-5   (Camden Large Print)

The text of this Large Print edition is unabridged.
Other aspects of the book may vary from the original edition.

Set in 16 pt. Plantin by Minnie B. Raven.

Printed in the United States on permanent paper.

British Library Cataloguing in Publication Data Available

Library of Congress Cataloging in Publication Data

Grey, Zane, 1872–1939.
   The young forester / by Zane Grey.
     p.   cm.
   ISBN 0-7838-0295-1 (lg. print : hc : alk. paper)
   1. Large type books.   I. Title.
[PS3513.R6545Y68   1998]
813'.52—dc21   98-25557

Contents

I.	Choosing a Profession	7
II.	The Man on the Train	18
III.	The Trail	28
IV.	Lost in the Forest	40
V.	The Sawmill	47
VI.	Dick Leslie, Ranger	56
VII.	Back to Holston	68
VIII.	The Lumbermen	74
IX.	Taken into the Mountains	83
X.	Escape	94
XI.	The Old Hunter	103
XII.	Bears	118
XIII.	The Cabin in the Forest	131
XIV.	A Prisoner.	145
XV.	The Fight	156
XVI.	The Forest's Greatest Foe	169
XVII.	The Back-Fire	184
XVIII.	Conclusion	196

I

Choosing a Profession

I loved outdoor life and hunting. Some way a grizzly bear would come in when I tried to explain forestry to my brother.

"Hunting grizzlies!" he cried. "Why, Ken, father says you've been reading dime novels."

"Just wait, Hal, till he comes out here. I'll show him that forestry isn't just bear-hunting."

My brother Hal and I were camping a few days on the Susquehanna River, and we had divided the time between fishing and tramping. Our camp was on the edge of a forest some eight miles from Harrisburg. The property belonged to our father, and he had promised to drive out to see us. But he did not come that day, and I had to content myself with winning Hal over to my side.

"Ken, if the governor lets you go to Arizona can't you ring me in?"

"Not this summer. I'd be afraid to ask him. But in another year I'll do it."

"Won't it be great? But what a long time to wait! It makes me sick to think of you out there riding mustangs and hunting bears and lions."

"You'll have to stand it. You're pretty much of a kid, Hal — not yet fourteen. Besides, I've graduated."

"Kid!" exclaimed Hal, hotly. "You're not such a Methuselah yourself! I'm nearly as big as you. I can ride as well and play ball as well, and I can beat you all —"

"Hold on, Hal! I want you to help me to persuade father, and if you get your temper up you'll like as not go against me. If he lets me go I'll bring you in as soon as I dare. That's a promise. I guess I know how much I'd like to have you."

"All right," replied Hal, resignedly. "I'll have to hold in, I suppose. But I'm crazy to go. And, Ken, the cowboys and lions are not all that interest me. I like what you tell me about forestry. But who ever heard of forestry as a profession?"

"It's just this way, Hal. The natural resources have got to be conserved, and the Government is trying to enlist intelligent young men in the work — particularly in the department of forestry. I'm not exaggerating when I say the prosperity of this country depends upon forestry."

I have to admit that I was repeating what I had read.

"Why does it? Tell me how," demanded Hal.

"Because the lumbermen are wiping out all the timber and never thinking of the future. They are in such a hurry to get rich that they'll leave their grandchildren only a desert. They cut and slash in every direction, and then fires come and the country is ruined. Our rivers depend upon the forests for water. The trees draw the rain; the leaves break it up and let it fall in mists and drippings; it seeps into the ground, and is held by the roots. If the trees are destroyed the rain rushes off on the surface and floods the rivers. The forests store up water, and they do good in other ways."

"We've got to have wood and lumber," said Hal.

"Of course we have. But there won't be any unless we go in for forestry. It's been practiced in Germany for three hundred years."

We spent another hour talking about it, and if Hal's practical sense, which he inherited from father, had not been offset by his real love for the forests I should have been discouraged. Hal was of an industrious turn of mind; he meant to make money, and anything that was good business appealed strongly to him. But, finally, he began to see what I was driving at; he admitted that there was something in the argument.

The late afternoon was the best time for fishing. For the next two hours our thoughts were of quivering rods and leaping bass.

"You'll miss the big bass this August," remarked Hal, laughing. "Guess you won't have all the sport."

"That's so, Hal," I replied, regretfully. "But we're talking as if it were a dead sure thing that I'm going West. Well, I only hope so."

What Hal and I liked best about camping — of course after the fishing — was to sit around the camp-fire. To-night it was more pleasant than ever, and when darkness fully settled down it was even thrilling. We talked about bears. Then Hal told of mountain-lions and the habit they have of creeping stealthily after hunters. There was a hoot-owl crying dismally up in the woods, and down by the edge of the river bright-green eyes peered at us from the darkness. When the wind came up and moaned through the trees it was not hard to imagine we were out in the wilderness. This had been a favorite game for Hal and me; only to-night there seemed some reality about it. From the way Hal whispered, and listened, and looked, he might very well have been expecting a visit from lions or, for that matter, even from Indians. Finally we went to bed. But our slumbers were broken. Hal often had nightmares even on ordinary nights, and on this one he moaned so much and thrashed about the tent so desperately that I knew the lions were after him.

I dreamed of forest lands with snow-capped peaks rising in the background; I dreamed of elk standing on the open ridges, of white-tailed deer trooping out of the hollows, of antelope browsing on the sage at the edge of the forests. Here was the broad track of a grizzly in the snow; there on a sunny crag lay a tawny mountain-lion asleep. The bronzed cowboy came in for his share, and the lone bandit played his part in a way to make me shiver. The great pines, the shady, brown trails, the sunlit glades, were as real to me as if I had been among them. Most vivid of all was the lonely forest at night and the camp-fire. I heard the sputter of the red embers and smelled the wood smoke; I peered into the dark shadows watching and listening for I knew not what.

On the next day early in the afternoon father appeared on the river road.

"There he is," cried Hal. "He's driving Billy. How he's coming!"

Billy was father's fastest horse. It pleased me immensely to see the pace, for father would not have been driving fast unless he were in a particularly good humor. And when he stopped on the bank above camp I could have shouted. He wore his corduroys as if he were ready for outdoor life. There was a smile on his face as he tied Billy, and, coming down, he poked into everything in camp and asked innumerable questions. Hal talked about the bass until I was afraid he would want to go fishing and postpone our forestry tramp in the woods. But presently he spoke directly to me.

"Well, Kenneth, are you going to come out with the truth about that Wild-West scheme of yours? Now that you've graduated you want a fling. You want to ride mustangs, to see cowboys, to hunt and shoot — all that sort of thing."

When father spoke in such a way it usually meant the defeat of my schemes. I grew cold all over.

"Yes, father, I'd like all that — But I mean business. I want to be a forest ranger. Let me

11

go to Arizona this summer. And in the fall I'd — I'd like to go to a school of forestry."

There! the truth was out, and my feelings were divided between relief and fear. Before father could reply I launched into a set speech upon forestry, and talked till I was out of breath.

"There's something in what you say," replied my father. "You've been reading up on the subject?"

"Everything I could get, and I've been trying to apply my knowledge in the woods. I love the trees. I'd love an outdoor life. But forestry won't be any picnic. A ranger must be able to ride and pack, make trail and camp, live alone in the woods, fight fire and wild beasts. Oh! It'd be great!"

"I dare say," said father, dryly; "particularly the riding and shooting. Well, I guess you'll make a good-enough doctor to suit me."

"Give me a square deal," I cried, jumping up. "Mayn't I have one word to say about my future? Wouldn't you rather have me happy and successful as a forester, even if there is danger, than just an ordinary, poor doctor? Let's go over our woodland. I'll prove that you are letting your forest run down. You've got sixty acres of hard woods that ought to be bringing a regular income. If I can't prove it, if I can't interest you, I'll agree to study medicine. But if I do you're to let me try forestry."

"Well, Kenneth, that's a fair proposition," returned father, evidently surprised at my earnestness. "Come on. We'll go up in the woods. Hal, I suppose he's won you over?"

"Ken's got a big thing in mind," replied Hal, loyally. "It's just splendid."

I never saw the long, black-fringed line of trees without joy in the possession of them and a desire to live among them. The sixty acres of timber land covered the whole of a swampy valley, spread over a rolling hill sloping down to the glistening river.

"Now, son, go ahead," said my father, as we clambered over a rail fence and stepped into the edge of shade.

"Well, father —" I began, haltingly, and could not collect my thoughts. Then we were in the cool woods. It was very still, there being only a faint rustling of leaves and the mellow note of a hermit-thrush. The deep shadows were lightened by shafts of sunshine which, here and there, managed to pierce the canopy of foliage. Somehow, the feeling roused by these things loosened my tongue.

"This is an old hard-wood forest," I began. "Much of the white oak, hickory, ash, maple, is virgin timber. These trees have reached maturity; many are dead at the tops; all of them should have been cut long ago. They make too dense a shade for the seedlings to survive. Look at that bunch of sapling maples. See how they reach up, trying to get to the light. They haven't a branch low down and the tops are thin. Yet maple is one of our hardiest trees. Growth has been

13

suppressed. Do you notice there are no small oaks or hickories just here? They can't live in deep shade. Here's the stump of a white oak cut last fall. It was about two feet in diameter. Let's count the rings to find its age — about ninety years. It flourished in its youth and grew rapidly, but it had a hard time after about fifty years. At that time it was either burned, or mutilated by a falling tree, or struck by lightning."

"Now, how do you make that out?" asked father, intensely interested.

"See the free, wide rings from the pith out to about number forty-five. The tree was healthy up to that time. Then it met with an injury of some kind, as is indicated by this black scar. After that the rings grew narrower. The tree struggled to live."

We walked on with me talking as fast as I could get the words out. I showed father a giant, bushy chestnut which was dominating all the trees around it, and told him how it retarded their growth. On the other hand, the other trees were absorbing nutrition from the ground that would have benefited the chestnut.

"There's a sinful waste of wood here," I said, as we climbed over and around the windfalls and rotting tree-trunks. "The old trees die and are blown down. The amount of rotting wood equals the yearly growth. Now, I want to show you the worst enemies of the trees. Here's a big white oak, a hundred and fifty years old. It's almost dead. See the little holes bored in the bark. They were made by a beetle. Look!"

I swung my hatchet and split off a section of bark. Everywhere in the bark and round the tree ran little dust-filled grooves. I pried out a number of tiny brown beetles, somewhat the shape of a pinching-bug, only very much smaller.

"There! You'd hardly think that that great tree was killed by a lot of little bugs, would you? They girdle the trees and prevent the sap from flowing."

I found an old chestnut which contained nests of the deadly white moth, and explained how it laid its eggs, and how the caterpillars that came from them killed the trees by eating the leaves. I showed how mice and squirrels injured the forest by eating the seeds.

"First I'd cut and sell all the matured and dead timber. Then I'd thin out the spreading trees that want all the light, and the saplings that grow too close together. I'd get rid of the beetles, and try to check the spread of caterpillars. For trees grow twice as fast if they are not choked or diseased. Then I'd keep planting seeds and shoots in the open places, taking care to favor the species best adapted to the soil, and cutting those that don't grow well. In this way we'll be keeping our forest while doubling its growth and value, and having a yearly income from it."

"Kenneth, I see you're in dead earnest about this business," said my father, slowly. "Before I came out here to-day I had been looking up the subject, and I believe, with you, that forestry really means the salvation of our country. I think you are really interested, and I've a mind not to oppose you."

"You'll never regret it. I'll learn; I'll work up. Then it's an outdoor life — healthy, free — why! all the boys I've told take to the idea. There's something fine about it."

"Forestry it is, then," replied he. "I like the promise of it, and I like your attitude. If you have learned so much while you were camping out here the past few summers it speaks well for you. But why do you want to go to Arizona?"

"Because the best chances are out West. I'd like to get a line on the National Forests there before I go to college. The work will be different; those Western forests are all pine. I've a friend, Dick Leslie, a fellow I used to fish with, who went West and is now a fire ranger in the new National Forest in Arizona — Penetier is the name of it. He has written me several times to come out and spend a while with him in the woods."

"Penetier? Where is that — near what town?"

"Holston. It's a pretty rough country, Dick says; plenty of deer, bears, and lions on his range. So I could hunt some while studying the forests. I think I'd be safe with Dick, even if it is wild out there."

"All right, I'll let you go. When you return we'll see about the college." Then he surprised me by drawing a letter from his pocket and handing it to me. "My friend, Mr. White, got this letter from the department at Washington. It may be of use to you out there."

So it was settled, and when father drove off homeward Hal and I went back to camp. It would have been hard to say which of us was the more excited. Hal did a war-dance round the camp-fire. I was glad, however, that he did not have the little twinge of remorse which I experienced, for I had not told him or father *all* that Dick had written about the wilderness of Penetier. I am afraid my mind was as much occupied with rifles and mustangs as with the study of forestry. But, though the adventure called most strongly to me, I knew I was sincere about the forestry end of it, and I resolved that I would never slight my opportunities. So, smothering conscience, I fell to the delight of making plans. I was for breaking camp at once, but Hal persuaded me to stay one more day. We talked for hours. Only one thing bothered me. Hal was jolly and glum by turns. He revelled in the plans for my outfit, but he wanted his own chance. A thousand times I had to repeat my promise, and the last thing he said before we slept was:

"Ken, you're going to ring me in next summer!"

II

The Man on the Train

Travelling was a new experience to me, and on the first night after I left home I lay awake until we reached Altoona. We rolled out of smoky Pittsburg at dawn, and from then on the only bitter drop in my cup of bliss was that the train flew so fast I could not see everything out of my window.

Four days to ride! The great Mississippi to cross, the plains, the Rocky Mountains, then the Arizona plateaus — a long, long journey with a wild pine forest at the end! I wondered what more any young fellow could have wished. With my face glued to the car window I watched the level country speed by.

There appeared to be one continuous procession of well-cultivated farms, little hamlets, and prosperous towns. What interested me most, of course, were the farms, for all of them had some kind of wood. We passed a zone of maple forests which looked to be more carefully kept than the others. Then I recognized that they were maple-sugar trees. The farmers had cleaned out the other species, and this primitive method of forestry had produced the finest maples it had ever been my good-fortune to see. Indiana was flatter than Ohio, not so well watered, and therefore less heavily timbered. I saw, with regret, that the woodland was being cut regularly, tree after tree, and stacked in cords for firewood.

At Chicago I was to change for Santa Fé, and finding my train in the station I climbed aboard. My car was a tourist coach. Father had insisted on buying a ticket for the California Limited, but I had argued that a luxurious Pullman was not exactly the thing for a prospective forester. Still I pocketed the extra money which I had assured him he need not spend for the first-class ticket.

The huge station, with its glaring lights and clanging bells, and the outspreading city, soon gave place to prairie land.

That night I slept little, but the very time I wanted to be awake — when we crossed the Mississippi — I was slumbering soundly, and so missed it.

"I'll bet I don't miss it coming back," I vowed.

The sight of the Missouri, however, somewhat repaid me for the loss. What a muddy, wide river! And I thought of the thousands of miles of country it drained, and of the forests there must be at its source. Then came the never-ending Kansas corn-fields. I do not know whether it was their length or their treeless monotony, but I grew tired looking at them.

From then on I began to take some notice of my fellow-travellers. The conductor proved to be an agreeable old fellow; and the train-boy, though I mistrusted his advances because he tried to sell me everything from chewing-gum to mining stock, turned out to be pretty good company. The negro porter had such a jolly voice and laugh that I talked to him whenever I got the chance. Then occasional passengers occupied the seat opposite me from town to town. They were much alike, all sunburned and loud-voiced, and it looked as though they had all bought their high boots and wide hats at the same shop.

The last traveller to face me was a very heavy man with a great bullet head and a shock of light hair. His blue eyes had a bold flash, his long mustache drooped, and there was something about him that I did not like. He wore a huge diamond in the bosom of his flannel shirt, and a leather watch-chain that was thick and strong enough to have held up a town-clock.

"Hot," he said, as he mopped his moist brow.

"Not so hot as it was," I replied.

"Sure not. We're climbin' a little. He's whistlin' for Dodge City now."

"Dodge City?" I echoed, with interest. The name brought back vivid scenes from certain yellow-backed volumes, and certain uncomfortable memories of my father's displeasure. "Isn't this the old cattle town where there used to be so many fights?"

"Sure. An' not so very long ago. Here, look out the window." He clapped his big hand on my knee; then pointed. "See that hill there.

Dead Man's Hill it was once, where they buried the fellers as died with their boots on."

I stared, and even stretched my neck out of the window.

"Yes, old Dodge was sure lively," he continued, as our train passed on. "I seen a little mix-up there myself in the early eighties. Five cow-punchers, friends they was, had been visitin' town. One feller, playful-like, takes another feller's quirt — that's a whip. An' the other feller, playful-like, says, 'Give it back.' Then they tussles for it, an' rolls on the ground. I was laughin', as was everybody, when, suddenly, the owner of the quirt thumps his friend. Both cowboys got up, slow, an' watchin' of each other. Then the first feller, who had started the play, pulls his gun. He'd hardly flashed it when they all pulls guns, an' it was some noisy an' smoky. In about five seconds there was five dead cow-punchers. Killed themselves, as you might say, just for fun. That's what life was worth in old Dodge."

After this story I felt more kindly disposed toward my travelling companion, and would have asked for more romances but the conductor came along and engaged him in conversation. Then my neighbor across the aisle, a young fellow not much older than myself, asked me to talk to him.

"Why, yes, if you like," I replied, in surprise. He was pale; there were red spots in his cheeks, and dark lines under his weary eyes.

"You look so strong and eager that it's done

21

me good to watch you," he explained, with a sad smile. "You see — I'm sick."

I told him I was very sorry, and hoped he would get well soon.

"I ought to have come West sooner," he replied, "but I couldn't get the money."

He looked up at me and then out of the window at the sun setting red across the plains. I tried to make him think of something beside himself, but I made a mess of it. The meeting with him was a shock to me. Long after dark, when I had stretched out for the night, I kept thinking of him and contrasting what I had to look forward to with his dismal future. Somehow it did not seem fair, and I could not get rid of the idea that I was selfish.

Next day I had my first sight of real mountains. And the Pennsylvania hills, that all my life had appeared so high, dwindled to nothing. At Trinidad, where we stopped for breakfast, I walked out on the platform sniffing at the keen thin air. When we crossed the Raton Mountains into New Mexico the sick boy got off at the first station, and I waved good-bye to him as the train pulled out. Then the mountains and the funny little adobe huts and the Pueblo Indians along the line made me forget everything else.

The big man with the heavy watch-chain was still on the train, and after he had read his newspaper he began to talk to me.

"This road follows the old trail that the gold-seekers took in forty-nine," he said. "We're comin' soon to a place, Apache Pass, where the Apaches used to ambush the wagon-trains. It's somewheres along here."

Presently the train wound into a narrow yellow ravine, the walls of which grew higher and higher.

"Them Apaches was the worst redskins ever in the West. They used to hide on top of this pass an' shoot down on the wagon-trains."

Later in the day he drew my attention to a mountain standing all by itself. It was shaped like a cone, green with trees almost to the summit, and ending in a bare stone peak that had a flat top.

"Starvation Peak," he said. "That name's three hundred years old, dates back to the time the Spaniards owned this land. There's a story about it that's likely true enough. Some Spaniards were attacked by Indians an' climbed to the peak, expectin' to be better able to defend themselves up there. The Indians camped below the peak an' starved the Spaniards. Stuck there till they starved to death! That's where it got its name."

"Those times you tell of must have been great," I said, regretfully. "I'd like to have been here then. But isn't the country all settled now? Aren't the Indians dead? There's no more fighting?"

"It's not like it used to be, but there's still warm places in the West. Not that the Indians break out often any more. But bad men are almost as bad, if not so plentiful, as when Billy the Kid run these parts. I saw two men shot an' another knifed jest before I went East to St. Louis."

"Where?"

"In Arizona. Holston is the station where I get off, an' it happened near there."

"Holston is where I'm going."

"You don't say. Well, I'm glad to meet you, young man. My name's Buell, an' I'm some known in Holston. What's your name?"

He eyed me in a sharp but not unfriendly manner, and seemed pleased to learn of my destination.

"Ward. Kenneth Ward. I'm from Pennsylvania."

"You haven't got the bugs. Any one can see that," he said, and as I looked puzzled he went on, with a smile, and a sounding rap on his chest: "Most young fellers as come out here have consumption. They call it bugs. I reckon you're seekin' your fortune."

"Yes, in a way."

"There's opportunities for husky youngsters out here. What're you goin' to rustle for, if I may ask?"

"I'm going in for forestry."

"Forestry? Do you mean lumberin'?"

"No. Forestry is rather the opposite of lumbering. I'm going in for Government forestry — to save the timber, not cut it."

It seemed to me he gave a little start of surprise; he certainly straightened up and looked at me hard.

"What's Government forestry?"

I told him to the best of my ability. He listened attentively enough, but thereafter he had not another word for me, and presently he went into the next car. I took his manner to be the Western abruptness that I had heard of, and presently forgot him in the scenery along the line. At Albuquerque I got off for a trip to a lunch-counter, and happened to take a seat next to him.

"Know anybody in Holston?" he asked.

As I could not speak because of a mouthful of sandwich I shook my head. For the moment I had forgotten about Dick Leslie, and when it did occur to me some Indians offering to sell me beads straightway drove it out of my mind again.

When I awoke the next day, it was to see the sage ridges and red buttes of Arizona. We were due at Holston at eight o'clock, but owing to a crippled engine the train was hours late. At last I fell asleep to be awakened by a vigorous shake.

"Holston. Your stop. Holston," the conductor was saying.

"All right," I said, sitting up and then making a grab for my grip. "We're pretty late, aren't we?"

"Six hours. It's two o'clock."

"Hope I can get a room," I said, as I followed him out on the platform. He held up his lantern so that the light would shine in my face.

"There's a hotel down the street a block or so. Better hurry and look sharp. Holston's not a safe place for a stranger at night."

I stepped off into a windy darkness. A lamp glimmered in the station window. By its light I made out several men, the foremost of whom had a dark, pointed face and glittering eyes. He wore a strange hat, and I knew from pictures I had seen that he was a Mexican. Then the bulky form of Buell loomed up. I called, but evidently he did not hear me. The men took his grips, and they moved away to disappear in the darkness. While I paused, hoping to see some one to direct me, the train puffed out, leaving me alone on the platform.

When I turned the corner I saw two dim lights, one far to the left, the other to the right, and the black outline of buildings under what appeared to be the shadow of a mountain. It was the quietest and darkest town I had ever struck.

I decided to turn toward the right-hand light, for the conductor had said "down the street." I set forth at a brisk pace, but the loneliness and strangeness of the place were rather depressing.

Before I had gone many steps, however, the sound of running water halted me, and just in the nick of time, for I was walking straight into a ditch. By peering hard into the darkness and feeling my way I found a bridge. Then it did not take long to reach the light. But it was a saloon, and not the hotel. One peep into it served to make me face about in double-quick time, and hurry in the opposite direction.

Hearing a soft footfall, I glanced over my shoulder, to see the Mexican that I had noticed at the station. He was coming from across the street. I wondered if he were watching me. He might be. My heart began to beat violently. Turning once again, I discovered that the fellow could not be seen in the pitchy blackness. Then I broke into a run.

III

The Trail

A short dash brought me to the end of the block; the side street was not so dark, and after I had crossed this open space I glanced backward.

Soon I sped into a wan circle of light, and, reaching a door upon which was a hotel sign, I burst in. Chairs were scattered about a bare office; a man stirred on a couch, and then sat up, blinking.

"I'm afraid — I believe some one's chasing me," I said.

He sat there eying me, and then drawled, sleepily:

"Thet ain't no call to wake a feller, is it?"

The man settled himself comfortably again, and closed his eyes.

"Say, isn't this a hotel? I want a room!" I cried.

"Up-stairs; first door." And with that the porter went to sleep in good earnest.

I made for the stairs, and, after a backward look into the street, I ran up. A smelly lamp shed a yellowish glare along a hall. I pushed open the first door, and, entering the room, bolted myself in. Then all the strength went out of my legs. When I sat down on the bed I was in a cold sweat and shaking like a leaf. Soon the weakness passed, and I moved about the room, trying to find a lamp or candle. Evidently the hotel, and, for that matter, the town of Holston, did not concern itself with such trifles as lights. On the instant I got a bad impression of Holston. I had to undress in the dark. When I pulled the window open a little at the top the upper sash slid all the way down. I managed to get it back, and tried raising the lower sash. It was very loose, but it stayed up. Then I crawled into bed.

Though I was tired and sleepy, my mind whirled so that I could not get to sleep. If I had been honest with myself I should have wished myself back home. Pennsylvania seemed a long way off, and the adventures that I had dreamed of did not seem so alluring, now that I was in a lonely room in a lonely, dark town. Buell had seemed friendly and kind — at least, in the beginning. Why had he not answered my call? The incident did not look well to me. Then I fell to wondering if the Mexican had really followed me. The first thing for me in the morning would be to buy a revolver. Then if any Mexicans —

A step on the tin roof outside frightened me stiff. I had noticed a porch, or shed, under my window. Some one must have climbed upon it. I stopped breathing to listen. For what seemed moments there was no sound. I wanted to think that the noise might have been made by a cat, but I couldn't. I was scared — frightened half to death.

If there had been a bolt on the window the matter would not have been so disturbing. I lay there a-quiver, eyes upon the gray window space of my room. Dead silence once more intervened. All I heard was the pound of my heart against my ribs.

Suddenly I froze at the sight of a black figure against the light of my window. I recognized the strange hat, the grotesque outlines. I was about to shout for help when the fellow reached down and softly began to raise the sash.

That made me angry. Jerking up in bed, I caught the heavy pitcher from the wash-stand and flung it with all my might.

Crash!

Had I smashed out the whole side of the room it could scarcely have made more noise. Accompanied by the clinking of glass and the creaking of tin, my visitor rolled off the roof. I waited, expecting an uproar from the other inmates of the hotel. No footstep, no call sounded within hearing. Once again the stillness settled down.

Then, to my relief, the gray gloom lightened, and dawn broke. Never had I been so glad to see the morning. While dressing I cast gratified glances at the ragged hole in the window. With the daylight my courage had returned, and I began to have a sort of pride in my achievement.

"If that fellow had known how I can throw a

baseball he'd have been careful," I thought, a little cockily.

I went down-stairs into the office. The sleepy porter was mopping the floor. Behind the desk stood a man so large that he made Buell seem small. He was all shoulders and beard.

"Can I get breakfast?"

"Nobody's got a half-hitch on you, has they?" he replied, jerking a monstrous thumb over his shoulder toward a door.

I knew the words half-hitch had something to do with a lasso, and I was rather taken back by the hotel proprietor's remark. The dining-room was more attractive than anything I had yet seen about the place: the linen was clean, and the ham and eggs and coffee that were being served to several rugged men gave forth a savory odor. But either the waiter was blind or he could not hear, for he paid not the slightest attention to me.

I waited, while trying to figure out the situation. Something was wrong, and, whatever it was, I guessed that it must be with me. After about an hour I got my breakfast. Then I went into the office, intending to be brisk, business-like, and careful about asking questions.

"I'd like to pay my bill, and also for a little damage," I said, telling what had happened.

"Somebody'll kill thet Greaser yet," was all the comment the man made.

I went outside, not knowing whether to be angry or amused with these queer people. In the

31

broad light of day Holston looked as bad as it had made me feel by night. All I could see were the station and freight-sheds, several stores with high, wide signs, glaringly painted, and a long block of saloons. When I had turned a street corner, however, a number of stores came into view with same three-storied brick buildings, and, farther out, many frame houses.

Moreover, this street led my eye to great snow-capped mountains, and I stopped short in my tracks, for I realized they were the Arizona peaks. Up the swelling slopes swept a black fringe that I knew to be timber. The mountains appeared to be close, but I knew that even the foot-hills were miles away. Penetier, I remembered from one of Dick's letters, was on the extreme northern slope, and it must be anywhere from forty to sixty miles off. The sharp, white peaks glistened in the morning sun; the air had a cool touch of snow and a tang of pine. I drew in a full breath, with a sense of satisfaction that I was in the West and would soon be among the pines.

Now I must buy my outfit and take the trail for Penetier. This I resolved to do with as few questions as possible. I never before was troubled by sensitiveness, but the fact had dawned upon me that I did not like being taken for a tenderfoot. So, with this in mind, I entered a general merchandise store.

It was very large, and full of hardware, harness, saddles, blankets — everything that cowboys and ranchmen use. Several men, two in shirt-sleeves, were chatting near the door. They saw me come in, and then, for all that it meant to them, I might as well not have been in existence at all. So I sat down to wait, determined to take Western ways and things as I found them. I sat there fifteen minutes by my watch. This was not so bad; but when a lanky, red-faced, leather-legged individual came in to be at once supplied with his wants, I began to get angry. I waited another five minutes, and still the friendly chatting went on. Finally I could stand it no longer.

"Will somebody wait on me?" I demanded.

One of the shirt-sleeved men leisurely got up and surveyed me.

"Do you want to buy something?" he drawled.

"Yes, I do."

"Why didn't you say so?"

The reply trembling on my lips was cut short by the entrance of Buell.

"Hello!" he said in a loud voice, shaking hands with me. "You've trailed into the right place. Smith, treat this lad right. It's guns an' knives an' lassoes he wants, I'll bet a hoss."

"Yes, I want an outfit," I said, much embarrassed. "I'm going to meet a friend out in Penetier, a ranger — Dick Leslie."

Buell started violently, and his eyes flashed. "Dick — Dick Leslie!" he said, and coughed loudly. "I know Dick. . . . So you're a friend of his'n? . . . Now, let me help you with the outfit."

Anything strange in Buell's manner was forgotten in the absorbing interest of my outfit. Father had given me plenty of money, so that I had but to choose. I had had sense enough to bring my old corduroys and boots, and I had donned them that morning. One after another I made my purchases — Winchester, revolver, holsters, ammunition, saddle, bridle, lasso, blanket. When I got so far, Buell said: "You'll need a mustang an' a pack-pony. I know a feller who's got jest what you want." And with that he led me out of the store.

"Now you take it from me," he went on, in a fatherly voice, "Holston people haven't got any use for Easterners. An' if you mention your business — forestry an' that — why, you wouldn't be safe. There's many in the lumberin' business here as don't take kindly to the Government. See! That's why I'm givin' you advice. Keep it to yourself an' hit the trail to-day, soon as you can. I'll steer you right."

I was too much excited to answer clearly; indeed, I hardly thanked him. However, he scarcely gave me the chance. He kept up his talk about the townspeople and their attitude toward Easterners until we arrived at a kind of stock-yard full of shaggy little ponies. The sight of them drove every other thought out of my head.

"Mustangs!" I exclaimed.

"Sure. Can you ride?"

"Oh yes. I have a horse at home. . . . What wiry little fellows! They're so wild-looking."

"You pick out the one as suits you, an' I'll

step into Cless's here. He's the man who owns this bunch."

It did not take me long to decide. A black mustang at once took my eye. When he had been curried and brushed he would be a little beauty. I was trying to coax him to me when Buell returned with a man.

"Thet your pick?" he asked, as I pointed. "Well, now, you're not so much of a tenderfoot. Thet's the best mustang in the lot. Cless, how much for him, an' a pack-pony an' pack-saddle?"

"I reckon twenty dollars'll make it square," replied the owner.

This nearly made me drop with amazement. I had only about seventy-five dollars left, and I had been very much afraid that I could not buy the mustang, let alone the pack-pony and saddle.

"Cless, send round to Smith for the lad's outfit, an' saddle up for him at once." Then he turned to me. "Now some grub, an' a pan or two."

Having camped before, I knew how to buy supplies. Buell, however, cut out much that I wanted, saying the thing to think of was a light pack for the pony.

"I'll hurry to the hotel and get my things," I said, "and meet you here. I'll not be a moment."

But Buell said it would be better for him to go with me, though he did not explain. He kept with me, still he remained in the office while I went up-stairs. Somehow this suited me, for I did not want him to see the broken window. I took a few things from my grip and rolled them in a bundle. Then I took a little leather case of odds and ends I had always carried when camping and slipped it into my pocket. Hurrying down-stairs I left my grip with the porter, wrote and mailed a postal card to my father, and followed the impatient Buell.

"You see, it's a smart lick of a ride to Penetier, an' I want you to get there before dark," he explained, kindly.

I could have shouted for very glee when I saw the black mustang saddled and bridled.

"He's well broke," said Cless. "Keep his bridle down when you ain't in the saddle. An' find a patch of grass fer him at night. The pony'll stick to him."

Cless fell to packing a lean pack-pony.

"Watch me do this," said he; "you'll hev trouble if you don't git the hang of the diamond-hitch."

I watched him set the little wooden criss-cross on the pony's back, throw the balance of my outfit (which he had tied up in a canvas) over the saddle, and then pass a long rope in remarkable turns and wonderful loops round pony and pack.

"What's the mustang's name?" I inquired.

"Never had any," replied the former owner.

"Then it's Hal." I thought how that name would please my brother at home.

"Climb up. Let's see if you fit the stirrups," said Cless. "Couldn't be better."

"Now, young feller, you can hit the trail," put in Buell, with his big voice. "An' remember what I told you. This country ain't got much use for a feller as can't look out for himself."

He opened the gate, and led my mustang into the road and quite some distance. The pony jogged along after us. Then Buell stopped with a finger outstretched.

"There, at the end of this street, you'll find a trail. Hit it an' stick to it. All the little trails leadin' into it needn't bother you."

He swept his hand round to the west of the mountain. The direction did not tally with the idea I had gotten from Dick's letter.

"I thought Penetier was on the north side of the mountains."

"Who said so?" he asked, staring. "Don't I know this country? Take it from me."

I thanked him, and, turning, with a light heart I faced the black mountain and my journey.

It was about ten o'clock when Hal jogged into a broad trail on the outskirts of Holston. A gray flat lay before me, on the other side of which began the slow rise of the slope. I could hardly contain myself. I wanted to run the mustang, but did not for the sake of the burdened pony. That sage-flat was miles wide, though it seemed so narrow. The back of the lower slope began to change to a dark green, which told me I was surely getting closer to the mountains, even if it did not seem so. The trail began to rise, and at last I reached the first pine-trees. They were a disappointment to me, being no larger than many of the white oaks at home, and stunted, with ragged dead tops. They proved to me that trees isolated from their fellows fare as poorly as trees overcrowded. Where pines grow closely, but not too closely, they rise straight and true, cleaning themselves of the low branches, and making good lumber, free of knots. Where they grow far apart, at the mercy of wind and heat and free to spread many branches, they make only gnarled and knotty lumber.

As I rode on the pines became slowly more numerous and loftier. Then, when I had surmounted what I took to be the first foot-hill, I came upon a magnificent forest. A little farther on the trail walled me in with great seamed trunks, six feet in diameter, rising a hundred feet before spreading a single branch.

Meanwhile my mustang kept steadily up the slow-rising trail, and the time passed. Either the grand old forest had completely bewitched me or the sweet smell of pine had intoxicated me, for as I rode along utterly content I entirely forgot about Dick and the trail and where I was heading. Nor did I come to my senses until Hal snorted and stopped before a tangled windfall.

Then I glanced down to see only the clean, brown pine-needles. There was no trail. Perplexed and somewhat anxious, I rode back a piece, expecting surely to cross the trail. But I did not. I went to the left and to the right, then circled in a wide curve. No trail! The forest about me seemed at once familiar and strange.

It was only when the long shadows began to creep under the trees that I awoke fully to the truth.

I had missed the trail! I was lost in the forest!

IV

Lost in the Forest

For a moment I was dazed. And then came panic. I ran up this ridge and that one, I rushed to and fro over ground which looked, whatever way I turned, exactly the same. And I kept saying, "I'm lost! I'm lost!" Not until I dropped exhausted against a pine-tree did any other thought come to me.

The moment that I stopped running about so aimlessly the panicky feeling left me. I remembered that for a ranger to be lost in the forest was an every-day affair, and the sooner I began that part of my education the better. Then it came to me how foolish I had been to get alarmed, when I knew that the general slope of the forest led down to the open country.

This put an entirely different light upon the matter. I still had some fears that I might not soon find Dick Leslie, but these I dismissed for the present, at least. A suitable place to camp for the night must be found. I led the mustang down into the hollows, keeping my eye sharp for grass. Presently I came to a place that was wet and soggy at the bottom, and, following this up for quite a way, I found plenty of grass and a pool of clear water.

Often as I had made camp back in the woods of Pennsylvania, the doing of it now was new. For this was not play; it was the real thing, and it made the old camping seem tame. I took the saddle off Hal and tied him with my lasso, making as long a halter as possible. Slipping the pack from the pony was an easier task than the getting it back again was likely to prove. Next I broke open a box of cartridges and loaded the Winchester. My revolver was already loaded, and hung on my belt. Remembering Dick's letters about the bears and mountain-lions in Penetier Forest, I got a good deal of comfort out of my weapons. Then I built a fire, and while my supper was cooking I scraped up a mass of pine-needles for a bed. Never had I sat down to a meal with such a sense of strange enjoyment.

But when I had finished and had everything packed away and covered, my mind began to wander in unexpected directions. Why was it that the twilight seemed to move under the giant pines and creep down the hollow? While I gazed the gray shadows deepened to black, and night came suddenly. My camp-fire seemed to give almost no light, yet close at hand the flickering gleams played hide-and-seek among the pines and chased up the straight tree trunks. The crackling of my fire and the light steps of the grazing mustangs only emphasized the silence of the forest. Then a low moaning from a distance gave me a chill. At first I had no idea what it was, but presently I thought it must be the wind in the pines. It bore no resemblance to any sound I had ever before heard in the woods. It would murmur from different parts of the forest; sometimes it would cease for a little, and then travel and swell toward me, only to die away again. But it rose steadily, with shorter intervals of silence, until the intermittent gusts swept through the tree-tops with a rushing roar. I had listened to the crash of the ocean surf, and the resemblance was a striking one.

Listening to this mournful wind with all my ears I was the better prepared for any lonesome cries of the forest; nevertheless, a sudden, sharp "Ki-yi-i!" seemingly right at my back, gave me a fright that sent my tongue to the roof of my mouth.

Fumbling at the hammer of my rifle, I peered into the black-streaked gloom of the forest. The crackling of dry twigs brought me to my feet. At the same moment the mustangs snorted. Something was prowling about just beyond the light. I thought of a panther. That was the only beast I could think of which had such an unearthly cry.

Then another howl, resembling that of a dog, and followed by yelps and barks, told me that I was being visited by a pack of coyotes. I spent the good part of an hour listening to their serenade. The wild, mournful notes sent quivers up my back. By-and-by they went away, and as my fire had burned down to a red glow and the night wind had grown cold I began to think of sleep.

But I was not sleepy. When I had stretched out on the soft bed of pine-needles with my rifle close by, and was all snug and warm under the heavy blanket, it seemed that nothing was so far away from me as sleep. The wonder of my situation kept me wide awake, my eyes on the dim huge pines and the glimmer of stars, and my ears open to the rush and roar of the wind, every sense alert. Hours must have passed as I lay there living over the things that had happened and trying to think out what was to come. At last, however, I rolled over on my side, and with my hand on the rifle and my cheek close to the sweet-smelling pine-needles I dropped asleep.

When I awoke the forest was bright and sunny.

"You'll make a fine forester," I said aloud, in disgust at my tardiness. Then began the stern business of the day. While getting breakfast I turned over in my mind the proper thing for me to do. Evidently I must pack and find the trail. The pony had wandered off into the woods, but was easily caught — a fact which lightened my worry, for I knew how dependent I was upon my mustangs. When I had tried for I do not know how long to get my pack to stay on the pony's back I saw where Mr. Cless had played a joke on me. All memory of the diamond-hitch had faded into utter confusion. First the pack fell over the off-side; next, on top of me; then the saddle slipped awry, and when I did get the pack to remain stationary upon the patient pony, how on earth to tie it there became more and more of a mystery. Finally, in sheer desperation, I ran round the pony, pulled, tugged, and knotted the lasso; more by luck than through sense I had accomplished something in the nature of the diamond-hitch.

I headed Hal up the gentle forest slope, and began the day's journey wherever chance might lead me. As confidence came, my enjoyment increased. I began to believe I could take care of myself. I reasoned out that, as the peaks were snow-capped, I should find water, and very likely game, up higher. Moreover, I might climb a foothill or bluff from which I could get my bearings.

It seemed to me that I passed more pine-trees than I could have imagined there were in the whole world. Miles and miles of pines! And in every mile they grew larger and ruggeder and farther apart, and so high that I could hardly see the tips. After a time I got out of the almost level forest into ground ridged and hollowed, and found it advisable to turn more to the right. On the sunny southern slopes I saw trees that dwarfed the ones on the colder and shady north sides. I also found many small pines and seedlings growing in warm, protected places. This showed me the value of the sun to a forest. Though I kept a lookout for deer or game of any kind, I saw nothing except some black squirrels with white tails. They were beautiful and very tame, and one was nibbling at what I concluded must have been a seed from a pine-cone.

Presently I fancied that I espied a moving speck far down through the forest glades. I stopped Hal, and, watching closely, soon made certain of it. Then it became lost for a time, but reappeared again somewhat closer. It was like a brown blur and scarcely moved. I reined Hal more to the right. Not for quite a while did I see the thing again, and when I did it looked so big and brown that I took up my Winchester. Then it disappeared once more.

I descended into a hollow, and tying Hal, I stole forward on foot, hoping by that means to get close to the strange object without being seen myself.

I waited behind a pine, and suddenly three horsemen rode across a glade not two hundred yards away. The foremost rider was no other than the Mexican whom I had reason to remember.

The huge trunk amply concealed me, but, nevertheless, I crouched down. How strange that I should run into that Mexican again! Where was he going? Had he followed me? Was there a trail?

As long as the three men were in sight I watched them. When the last brown speck had flitted and disappeared far away in the forest I retraced my steps to my mustang, pondering upon this new turn in my affairs.

"Things are bound to happen to me," I concluded, "and I may as well make up my mind to that."

While standing beside Hal, undecided as to my next move, I heard a whistle. It was faint, perhaps miles away, yet unmistakably it was the whistle of an engine. I wondered if the railroad turned round this side of the peaks. Mounting Hal, I rode down the forest to the point where I had seen the men, and there came upon a trail. I proceeded along this in the direction the men had taken. I had come again to the slow-rising level that I had noted earlier in my morning's journey. After several miles a light or opening in the forest ahead caused me to use more caution. As I rode forward I saw a vast area of tree-tops far below, and then I found myself on the edge of a foot-hill.

Right under me was a wide, yellow, bare spot, miles across, a horrible slash in the green forest, and in the middle of it, surrounded by stacks on stacks of lumber, was a great sawmill.

I stared in utter amazement. A sawmill on Penetier! Even as I gazed a train of fresh-cut lumber trailed away into the forest.

V

The Sawmill

In my surprise I almost forgot the Mexican. Then I thought that if Dick were there the Mexican would be likely to have troubles of his own. I remembered Dick's reputation as a fighter.

But suppose I did not find Dick at the sawmill? This part of the forest was probably owned by private individuals, for I couldn't imagine Government timber being cut in this fashion. So I tied Hal and the pony amidst a thick clump of young pines, and, leaving all my outfit except my revolver, I struck out across the slash.

No second glance was needed to tell that the lumbering here was careless and without thought for the future. It had been a clean cut, and what small saplings had escaped the saw had been crushed by the dropping and hauling of the large pines. The stumps were all about three feet high, and that meant the waste of many thousands of feet of good lumber. Only the straight, unbranched trunks had been used. The tops of the pines had not been lopped, and lay where they had fallen. It was a wilderness of yellow brush, a dry jungle. The smell of pine was so powerful that I could hardly breathe. Fire must inevitably complete this work of ruin; already I was forester enough to see that.

Presently the trail crossed a railroad track which appeared to have been hastily constructed. Swinging along at a rapid step on the ties I soon reached the outskirts of the huge stacks of lumber; I must have walked half a mile between two yellow walls. Then I entered the lumber-camp.

It was even worse-looking than the slash. Rows of dirty tents, lines of squatly log-cabins, and many flat-board houses clustered around an immense sawmill. Evidently I had arrived at the noon hour, for the mill was not running, and many rough men were lounging about smoking pipes. At the door of the first shack stood a fat, round-faced negro wearing a long, dirty apron.

"Is Dick Leslie here?" I asked.

"I dunno if Dick's come in yet, but I 'specks him," he replied. "Be you the young gent Dick's lookin' fer from down East?"

"Yes."

"Come right in, sonny, come right in an' eat. Dick allus eats with me, an' he has spoke often 'bout you." He led me in, and seated me at a bench where several men were eating. They were brawny fellows, clad in overalls and undershirts, and one, who spoke pleasantly to me, had sawdust on his bare arms and even in his hair. The cook set before me a bowl of soup, a plate of beans, pot-roast, and coffee, all of which I attacked with a good appetite. Presently the men finished their meal and went outside, leaving me alone with the cook.

"Many men on this job?" I asked.

"More'n a thousand. Buell's runnin' two shifts, day an' night."

"Buell? Does he own this land?"

"No. He's only the agent of a 'Frisco lumber company, an' the land belongs to the Government. Buell's sure slashin' the lumber off, though. Two freight-trains of lumber out every day."

"Is this Penetier Forest?" I queried, carelessly, but I had begun to think hard.

"Sure."

I wanted to ask questions, but thought it wiser to wait. I knew enough already to make out that I had come upon the scene of a gigantic lumber steal. Buell's strange manner on the train, at the station, and his eagerness to hurry me out of Holston now needed no more explanation. I began to think the worst of him.

"Did you see a Mexican come into camp?" I inquired of the negro.

"Sure. Greaser got here this mornin'."

"He tried to rob me in Holston."

" 'Tain't nothin' new fer Greaser. He's a thief, but I never heerd of him holdin' anybody up. No nerve 'cept to knife a feller in the back."

"What'll I do if I meet him here?"

"Slam him one! You're a strappin' big lad. Slam him one, an' flash your gun on him. Greaser's a coward. I seen a young feller he'd cheated make him crawl. Anyway, it'll be all day with him when Dick finds out he tried to rob you. An' say, stranger, if a feller stays sober, this camp's safe enough in daytime, but at night, drunk or sober, it's a tough place."

Before I had finished eating a shrill whistle from the sawmill called the hands to work; soon it was followed by the rumble of machinery and the sharp singing of a saw.

I set out to see the lumber-camp, and although I stepped forth boldly, the truth was that with all my love for the Wild West I would have liked to be at home. But here I was, and I determined not to show the white feather.

I passed a row of cook-shacks like the one I had been in, and several stores and saloons. The lumber-camp was a little town. A rambling log-cabin attracted me by reason of the shaggy mustangs standing before it and the sounds of mirth within. A peep showed me a room with a long bar, where men and boys were drinking. I heard the rattle of dice and the clink of silver. Seeing the place was crowded, I thought I might find Dick there, so I stepped inside. My entrance was unnoticed, so far as I could tell; in fact, there seemed no reason why it should be otherwise, for, being roughly dressed, I did not look very different from the many young fellows there. I scanned all the faces, but did not see Dick's, nor, for that matter, the Mexican's. Both disappointed and relieved, I turned away, for the picture of low dissipation was not attractive.

The hum of the great sawmill drew me like a

magnet. I went out to the lumber-yard at the back of the mill, where a trestle slanted down to a pond full of logs. A train loaded with pines had just pulled in, and dozens of men were rolling logs off the flat-cars into a canal. At stations along the canal stood others pike-poling the logs toward the trestle, where an endless chain caught them with sharp claws and hauled them up. Half-way from the ground they were washed clean by a circle of water-spouts.

I walked up the trestle and into the mill. The noise almost deafened me. High above all other sounds rose the piercing song of the saw, and the short intervals when it was not cutting were filled with a thunderous crash that jarred the whole building. After a few confused glances I got the working order into my head, and found myself in the most interesting place I had ever seen.

As the stream of logs came up into the mill the first log was shunted off the chain upon a carriage. Two men operated this carriage by levers, one to take the log up to the saw, and the other to run it back for another cut. The run back was very swift. Then a huge black iron head butted up from below and turned the log over as easily as if it had been a straw. This was what made the jar and crash. On the first cut the long strip of bark went to the left and up against five little circular saws. Then the five pieces slipped out of sight down chutes. When the log was trimmed a man stationed near the

51

huge band-saw made signs to those on the carriage, and I saw that they got from him directions whether to cut the log into timbers, planks, or boards. The heavy timbers, after leaving the saw, went straight down the middle of the mill, the planks went to the right, the boards in another direction. Men and boys were everywhere, each with a lever in hand. There was not the slightest cessation of the work. And a log forty feet long and six feet thick, which had taken hundreds of years to grow, was cut up in just four minutes.

The place fascinated me. I had not dreamed that a sawmill could be brought to such a pitch of mechanical perfection, and I wondered how long the timber would last at that rate of cutting. The movement and din tired me, and I went outside upon a long platform. Here workmen caught the planks and boards as they came out, and loaded them upon trucks which were wheeled away. This platform was a world in itself. It sent arms everywhere among the piles of lumber, and once or twice I was as much lost as I had been up in the forest.

While turning into one of these byways I came suddenly upon Buell and another man. They were standing near a little house of weather-strips, evidently an office, and were in their shirt-sleeves. They had not seen or heard me. I dodged behind a pile of planks, intending to slip back the way I had come. Before I could move Buell's voice rooted me to the spot.

"His name's Ward. Tall, well-set lad. I put Greaser after him the other night, hopin' to scare him back East. But nix!"

"Well, he's here now — to study forestry! Ha! ha!" said the other.

"You're sure the boy you mean is the one I mean?"

"Greaser told me so. And this boy is Leslie's friend."

"That's the worst of it," replied Buell, impatiently. "I've got Leslie fixed as far as this lumber deal is concerned, but he won't stand for any more. He was harder to fix than the other rangers, an' he's grouchy now. I'm afraid of him."

"You shouldn't have let the boy get here."

"Stockton, I tried to prevent it. I put Greaser with Bud an' Bill on his trail. They didn't find him, an' now here he turns up."

"Maybe he can be fixed."

"Not if I know my business, he can't; take that from me. This kid is straight. He'll queer my deal in a minute if he gets wise. Mind you, I'm gettin' leery of Washington. We've seen about the last of these lumber deals. If I can pull this one off I'll quit; all I want is a little more time. Then I'll fire the slash, an' that'll cover tracks."

"Buell, I wouldn't want to be near Penetier when you light that fire. This forest will burn like tinder."

"It's a whole lot I care then. Let her burn. Let the Government put out the fire. Now, what's to be done about this boy?"

"I think I'd try to feel him out. Maybe he can be fixed. Boys who want to be foresters can't be rich. Failing that — you say he's a kid who wants to hunt and shoot — get some one to take him up on the mountain."

"See here, Stockton. This young Ward will see the timber is bein' cut clean. If it was only a little patch I wouldn't mind. But this slash an' this mill! He'll know. More'n that, he'll tell Leslie about the Mexican. Dick's no fool. We're up against it."

"It's risky, Buell. You remember the ranger up in Oregon."

"Then we are to fall down on this deal all because of a fresh tenderfoot kid?" demanded Buell.

"Not so loud. . . . We'll not fall down. But caution — use caution. You made a mistake in trusting so much to the Greaser."

"I know, an' I'm afraid of Leslie. An' that other fire-ranger, Jim Williams, he's a Texan, an' a bad man. The two of them could about trim up this camp. They'll both fight for the boy; take that from me."

"We are sure up against it. Think now, and think quick."

"First, I'll try to fix the boy. If that won't work . . . we'll kidnap him. Then we'll take no chances with Leslie. There's a cool two hundred an' fifty thousand in this deal for us, an' we're goin' to get it."

With that Buell went into his office and closed the door; the other man, Stockton, walked briskly down the platform. I could not resist peeping from my hiding-place as he passed. He was tall and had a red beard, which would enable me to recognize him if we met.

I waited there for some little time. Then I saw that by squeezing between two piles of lumber I could reach the other side of the platform. When I reached the railing I climbed over, and, with the help of braces and posts, soon got to where I could drop down. Once on the ground I ran along under the platform until I saw a lane that led to the street. My one thought was to reach the cabin where the negro cook stayed and ask him if Dick Leslie had come to camp. If he had not arrived, then I intended to make a bee-line for my mustang.

VI

Dick Leslie, Ranger

Which end of the street I entered I had no idea. The cabins were all alike, and in my hurry I would have passed the cook's shack had it not been for the sight of a man standing in the door. That stalwart figure I would have known anywhere.

"Dick!" I cried, rushing at him.

What Dick's welcome was I did not hear, but judging from the grip he put on my shoulders and then on my hands, he was glad to see me.

"Ken, blessed if I'd have known you," he said, shoving me back at arm's-length. "Let's have a look at you. . . . Grown! Say, but you're a husky lad!"

While he was looking at me I returned the scrutiny with interest. Dick had always been big, but now he seemed wider and heavier. Among these bronzed Westerners he appeared pale, but that was only on account of his fair skin.

"Ken, didn't you get my letter — the one telling you not to come West yet a while?"

"No," I replied, blankly. "The last one I got was in May — about the middle. I have it with me. You certainly asked me to come then. . . . Dick, don't you want me now?"

56

Plain it was that my friend felt uncomfortable; he shifted from one foot to another, and a cloud darkened his brow. But his blue eyes burned with a warm light as he put his hand on my shoulder.

"Ken, I'm glad to see you," he said, earnestly. "It's like getting a glimpse of home. But I wrote you not to come. Conditions have changed — there's something doing here — I'll —"

"You needn't explain, Dick," I replied, gravely. "I know. Buell and —" I waved my hand from the sawmill to the encircling slash.

Dick's face turned a fiery red. I believed that was the only time Dick Leslie ever failed to look a fellow in the eye.

"Ken! . . . You're on," he said, recovering his composure. "Well, wait till you hear — Hello! here's Jim Williams, my pardner."

A clinking of spurs accompanied a soft step.

"Jim, here's Ken Ward, the kid pardner I used to have back in the States," said Dick. "Ken, you know Jim."

If ever I knew anything by heart it was what Dick had written me about this Texan, Jim Williams.

"Ken, I shore am glad to see yu," drawled Jim, giving my hand a squeeze that I thought must break every bone in it.

Though Jim Williams had never been described to me, my first sight of him fitted my own ideas. He was tall and spare; his weather-beaten face seemed set like a dark mask; only his eyes moved, and they had a quivering alertness and a brilliancy that made them hard to look into. He wore a wide sombrero, a blue flannel shirt with a double row of big buttons, overalls, top-boots with very high heels, and long spurs. A heavy revolver swung at his hip, and if I had not already known that Jim Williams had fought Indians and killed bad men, I should still have seen something that awed me in the look of him.

I certainly felt proud to be standing with those two rangers, and for the moment Buell and all his crew could not have daunted me.

"Hello! what's this?" inquired Dick, throwing back my coat; and, catching sight of my revolver, he ejaculated: "Ken Ward!"

"Wal, Ken, if yu-all ain't packin' a gun!" said Jim, in his slow, careless drawl. "Dick, he shore is!"

It was now my turn to blush.

"Yes, I've got a gun," I replied, "and I ought to have had it the other night."

"How so?" inquired Dick, quickly.

It did not take me long to relate the incident of the Mexican.

Dick looked like a thunder-cloud, but Jim swayed and shook with laughter.

"Yu knocked him off the roof? Wal, thet shore is dee-lightful. It shore is!"

"Yes; and, Dick," I went on, breathlessly, "the Greaser followed me, and if I hadn't missed the trail, I don't know what would have happened.

Anyway, he got here first."

"The Greaser trailed you?" interrupted Dick, sharply.

When I replied he glanced keenly at me. "How do you know?"

"I suspected it when I saw him with two men in the forest. But now I know it."

"How?"

"I heard Buell tell Stockton he had put the Greaser on my trail."

"Buell — Stockton!" exclaimed Dick. "What'd they have to do with the Greaser?"

"I met Buell on the train. I told him I had come West to study forestry. Buell's afraid I'll find out about this lumber steal, and he wants to shut my mouth."

Dick looked from me to Jim, and Jim slowly straightened his tall form. For a moment neither spoke. Dick's white face caused me to look away from him. Jim put a hand on my arm.

"Ken, yu shore was lucky; yu shore was."

"I guess he doesn't know how lucky," added Dick, somewhat huskily. "Come on, we'll look up the Mexican."

"It shore is funny how bad I want to see thet Greaser."

Dick's hard look and tone were threatening enough, yet they did not affect me so much as the easy, gay manner of the Texan. Little cold quivers ran over me, and my knees knocked together. For the moment my animosity toward the Mexican vanished, and with it the old hunger to be in the thick of Wild Western life. I was afraid that I was going to see a man killed without being able to lift a hand to prevent it.

The rangers marched me between them down the street and into the corner saloon. Dick held me half behind him with his left hand while Jim sauntered ahead. Strangest of all the things that had happened was the sudden silencing of the noisy crowd.

The Mexican was not there. His companions, Bud and Bill, as Buell had called them, were sitting at a table, and as Jim Williams walked into the centre of the room they slowly and gradually rose to their feet. One was a swarthy man with evil eyes and a scar on his cheek; the other had a brick-red face and a sandy mustache with a vicious curl. Neither seemed to be afraid, only cautious.

"We're all lookin' for thet Greaser friend of yourn," drawled Jim. "I shore want tu see him bad."

"He's gone, Williams," replied one. "Was in somethin' of a rustle, an' didn't leave no word."

"Wal, I reckon he's all we're lookin' for this pertickler minnit."

Jim spoke in a soft, drawling voice, and his almost expressionless tone seemed to indicate pleasant indifference; still, no one could have been misled by it, for the long, steady gaze he gave the men and his cool presence that held the room quiet meant something vastly different. No reply was offered. Bud and Bill sat down, evidently to resume their card-playing. The uneasy silence broke to a laugh, then to subdued voices, and finally the clatter and hum began again. Dick led me outside, where we were soon joined by Jim.

"He's holed up," suggested Dick.

"Shore. I don't take no stock in his hittin' the trail. He's layin' low."

"Let's look around a bit, anyhow."

Dick took me back to the cook's cabin and, bidding me remain inside, strode away. I heard footsteps so soon after his departure that I made certain he had returned, but the burly form which blocked the light in the cabin door was not Dick's. I was astounded to recognize Buell.

"Hello!" he said, in his blustering voice. "Heard you had reached camp, an' have been huntin' you up."

I greeted him pleasantly enough — more from surprise than from a desire to mislead him. It seemed to me then that a child could have read Buell. He had an air of suppressed excitement; there was a glow on his face and a kind of daring flash in his eyes. He seemed too eager, too glad to see me.

"I've got a good job for you," he went on, glibly. "Jest what you want, an' you're jest what I need. Come into my office an' help me. There'll be plenty of outside work — measurin' lumber, markin' trees, an' such."

"Why, Mr. Buell — I — you see, Dick — he might not —"

I hesitated, not knowing how to proceed. But at my halting speech Buell became even more smiling and voluble.

"Dick? Oh, Dick an' I stand all right; take thet from me. Dick'll agree to what I want. I need a young feller bad. Money's no object. You're a bright youngster. You'll look out for my interests. Here!" He pulled out a large wad of greenbacks, and then spoke in a lower voice. "You understand that money cuts no ice 'round this camp. We've a big deal. We need a smart young feller. There's always some little irregularities about these big timber deals out West. But you'll wear blinkers, an' make some money while you're studyin' forestry. See?"

"Irregularities? What kind of irregularities?"

For the life of me I could not keep a little scorn out of my question. Buell slowly put the bills in his pocket while his eyes searched mine. I could not control my rising temper.

"You mean you want to fix me?"

He made no answer, and his face stiffened.

"You mean you want to buy my silence, shut my mouth about this lumber steal?"

He drew in his breath audibly, yet still he did not speak. Either he was dull of comprehension or else he was astonished beyond words. I knew I was mad to goad him like that, but I could not help it. I grew hot with anger, and the more clearly I realized that he had believed he could "fix" me with his dirty money the hotter I got.

"You told Stockton you were leary of Washington, and were afraid I'd queer your big deal. . . . Well, Mr. Buell, that's exactly what I'm going to do — queer it!"

He went black in the face, and, cursing horribly, grasped me by the arm. I struggled, but I could not loose that iron hand. Suddenly I felt a violent wrench that freed me. Then I saw Dick swing back his shoulder and shoot out his arm. He knocked Buell clear across the room, and when the man fell I thought the cabin was coming down in the crash. He appeared stunned, for he groped about with his hands, found a chair, and, using it as a support, rose to his feet, swaying unsteadily.

"Leslie, I'll get you for this — take it from me," he muttered.

Dick's lips were tight, and he watched Buell with flaming eyes. The lumberman lurched out of the door, and we heard him cursing after he had disappeared. Then Dick looked at me with no little disapproval.

"What did you say to make Buell wild like that?"

I told Dick, word for word. First he looked dumfounded, then angry, and he ended up with a grim laugh.

"Ken, you're sure bent on starting something, as Jim would say. You've started it all right. And Jim'll love you for it. But I'm responsible to your mother. Ken, I remember your mother — and you're going back home."

"Dick!"

63

"You're going back home as fast as I can get you to Holston and put you on a train, that's all."

"I won't go!" I cried.

Without any more words Dick led me down the street to a rude corral; here he rapidly saddled and packed his horses. The only time he spoke was when he asked me where I had tied my mustangs. Soon we were hurrying out through the slash toward the forest. Dick's troubled face kept down my resentment, but my heart grew like lead. What an ending to my long-cherished trip to the West! It had lasted two days. The disappointment seemed more than I could bear.

We found the mustangs as I had left them, and the sight of Hal and the feeling of the saddle made me all the worse. We did not climb the foot-hill by the trail which the Mexican had used, but took a long, slow ascent far round to the left. Dick glanced back often, and when we reached the top he looked again in a way to convince me that he had some apprehensions of being followed.

Twilight of that eventful day found us pitching camp in a thickly timbered hollow. I could not help dwelling on how different my feelings would have been if this night were but the beginning of many nights with Dick. It was the last, and the more I thought about it the more wretched I grew. Dick rolled in his blanket without saying even good-night, and I lay there watching the veils and shadows of firelight flicker on the pines, and listening to the wind. Gradually the bitterness seemed to go away; my body relaxed and sank into the soft, fragrant pine-needles; the great shadowy trees mixed with the surrounding darkness. When I awoke it was broad daylight, and Dick was shaking my arm.

"Hunt up the horses while I get the grub ready," he said, curtly.

As the hollow was carpeted with thick grass our horses had not strayed. I noticed that here the larger trees had been cut, and the forest resembled a fine park. In the sunny patches seedlings were sprouting, many little bushy pines were growing, and the saplings had sufficient room and light to prosper. I commented to Dick upon the difference between this part of Penetier and the hideous slash we had left.

"There were a couple of Government markers went through here and marked the timber to be cut," said Dick.

"Was the timber cut in the mill I saw?"

"No. Buell's just run up that mill. The old one is out here a ways, nearer Holston."

"Is it possible, Dick, that any of those loggers back there don't know the Government is being defrauded?"

"Ken, hardly any of them know it, and they wouldn't care if they did. You see, this forest-preserve business is new out here. Formerly the lumbermen bought so much land and cut over it — skinned it. Two years ago, when the Na-

65

tional Forests were laid out, the lumbering men — that is, the loggers, sawmill hands, and so on — found they did not get as much employment as formerly. So generally they're sore on the National Forest idea."

"But, Dick, if they understand the idea of forestry they'd never oppose it."

"Maybe. I don't understand it too well myself. I can fight fire — that's my business; but this ranger work is new. I doubt if the Westerners will take to forestry. There've been some shady deals all over the West because of it. Buell, now, he's a timber shark. He bought so much timber from the Government, and had the markers come in to mark the cut; then after they were gone, he rushed up a mill and clapped on a thousand hands."

"And the rangers stand for it? Where'll their jobs be when the Government finds out?"

"I was against it from the start. So was Jim, particularly. But the other rangers persuaded us."

It began to dawn upon me that Dick Leslie might, after all, turn out to be good soil in which to plant some seeds of forestry. I said no more then, as we were busy packing for the start, but when we had mounted I began to talk. I told him all I had learned about trees, how I loved them, and how I had determined to devote my life to their study, care, and development. As we rode along under the wide-spreading pines I illustrated my remarks by every example I could possibly use. The more I talked the more interested Dick became, and this spurred me on. Perhaps I exaggerated, but my conscience never pricked me. He began to ask questions.

We reached a spring at midday, and halted for a rest. I kept on pleading, and presently I discovered, to my joy, that I had made a strong impression upon Dick. It seemed a strange thing for me to be trying to explain forestry to a forest ranger, but so it was.

"Ken, it's all news to me. I've been on Penetier about a year, and I never heard a word of what you've been telling me. My duties have been the practical ones that any woodsman knows. Jim and the other rangers — why, they don't know any more than I. It's a great thing, and I've queered my chance with the Government."

"No, you haven't — neither has Jim — not if you'll be straight from now on. You can't keep faith with Buell. He tried to kidnap me. That lets you out. We'll spoil Buell's little deal and save Penetier. A letter to father will do it. He has friends in the Forestry Department at Washington. Dick, what do you say? It's not too late!"

The dark shade lifted from the ranger's face, and he looked at me with the smile of the old fishing days.

"Say? I say yes!" he exclaimed, in ringing voice. "Ken, you've made a man of me!"

VII

Back to Holston

Soon we were out of the forest, and riding across the sage-flat with Holston in sight. Both of us avoided the unpleasant subject of my enforced home-going. Evidently Dick felt cut up about it, and it caused me such a pang that I drove it from my mind. Toward the end of our ride Dick began again to talk of forestry.

"Ken, it's mighty interesting — all this you've said about trees. Some of the things are so simple that I wonder I didn't hit on them long ago; in fact, I knew a lot of what you might call forestry, but the scientific ideas — they stump me. Now, what you said about a pine-tree cleaning itself — come back at me with that."

"Why, that's simple enough, Dick," I answered. "Now, say here we have a clump of pine saplings. They stand pretty close — close enough to make dense shade, but not too crowded. The shade has prevented the lower branches from producing leaves. As a consequence these branches die. Then they dry, rot, and fall off, so when the trees mature they are clean-shafted. They have fine, clear trunks. They have cleaned themselves, and so make the best of lumber, free from knots."

So our talk went on. Once in town I was impatient to write to my father, for we had decided that we would not telegraph. Leaving our horses in Cless's corral, we went to the hotel and proceeded to compose the letter. This turned out more of a task than we had bargained for. But we got it finished at last, not forgetting to put in a word for Jim Williams, and then we both signed it.

"There!" I cried. "Dick, something will be doing round Holston before many days."

"That's no joke, you can bet," replied Dick, wiping his face. "Ken, it's made me sweat just to see that letter start East. Buell is a tough sort, and he'll make trouble. Well, he wants to steer clear of Jim and me."

After that we fell silent, and walked slowly back toward Cless's corral. Dick's lips were closed tight, and he did not look at me. Evidently he did not intend to actually put me aboard a train, and the time for parting had come. He watered his horses at the trough, and fussed over his pack and fumbled with his saddle-girths. It looked to me as though he had not the courage to say good-bye.

"Ken, it didn't look so bad — so mean till now," he said. "I'm all broken up. . . . To get you way out here! — Oh! what's the use? I'm mighty sorry. . . . Good-bye — maybe —"

He broke off suddenly, and, wringing my hand, he vaulted into the saddle. He growled at his pack-pony, and drove him out of the corral.

Then he set off at a steady trot down the street toward the open country.

It came to me in a flash, as I saw him riding farther and farther away, that the reason my heart was not broken was because I did not intend to go home. Dick had taken it for granted that I would board the next train for the East. But I was not going to do anything of the sort. To my amaze I found my mind made up on that score. I had no definite plan, but I was determined to endure almost anything rather than give up my mustang and outfit.

"It's shift for myself now," I thought, soberly. "I guess I can make good. . . . I'm going back to Penetier."

Even in the moment of impulse I knew how foolish this would be. But I could not help it. That forest had bewitched me. I meant to go back to it.

"I'll stay away from the sawmill," I meditated, growing lighter of heart every minute. "I'll keep out of sight of the lumbermen. I'll go higher up on the mountain, and hunt, and study the trees. . . . I'll do it."

Whereupon I marched off at once to a store and bought the supply of provisions that Buell had decided against when he helped me with my outfit. This addition made packing the pony more of a problem than ever, but I contrived to get it all on to my satisfaction. It was nearing sunset when I rode out of Holston this second time. The sage-flat was bare and gray. Dick had long since reached the pines, and would probably make camp at the spring where we had stopped for lunch. I certainly did not want to catch up with him, but as there was small chance of that, it caused me no concern.

Shortly after sunset twilight fell, and it was night when I reached the first pine-trees. Still, as the trail was easily to be seen, I kept on, for I did not want to camp without water. The forest was very dark, in some places like a huge black tent, and I had not ridden far when the old fear of night, the fancy of things out there in the darkness, once more possessed me. It made me angry. Why could I not have the same confidence that I had in the daytime? It was impossible. The forest was full of moving shadows. When the wind came up to roar in the pine-tips it was a relief because it broke the silence.

I began to doubt whether I could be sure of locating the spring, and I finally decided to make camp at once. I stopped Hal, and had swung my leg over the pommel when I saw a faint glimmer of light far ahead. It twinkled like a star, but was not white and cold enough for a star.

"That's Dick's camp-fire," I said. "I'll have to stop here. Maybe I'm too close now."

I pondered the question. The blaze was a long way off, and I concluded I could risk camping on the spot, provided I did not make a fire. Accordingly I dismounted, and was searching for a suitable place when I happened to think that the camp-fire might not be Dick's, after all. Perhaps Buell had sent the Mexican with Bud and Bill on my trail again. This would not do. But I did not want to go back or turn off the trail.

"I'll slip up and see who it is," I decided.

The idea pleased me; however, I did not yield to it without further consideration. I had a clear sense of responsibility. I knew that from now on I should be called upon to reason out many perplexing things. I did not want to make any mistakes. So I tied Hal and the pack-pony to a bush fringing the trail, and set off through the forest.

It dawned upon me presently that the camp-fire was much farther away than it appeared. Often it went out of sight behind trees. By degrees it grew larger and larger. Then I slowed down and approached more cautiously. Once when the trees obscured it I travelled some distance without getting a good view of it. Passing down into a little hollow I lost it again. When I climbed out I hauled up short with a sharp catch of my breath. There were several figures moving around the camp-fire. I had stumbled on a camp that surely was not Dick Leslie's.

The ground was as soft as velvet, and my footsteps gave forth no sound. When the wind lulled I paused behind a tree and waited for another gusty roar. I kept very close to the trail, for that was the only means by which I could return to my horses. I felt the skin tighten on my face. Suddenly, as I paused, I heard angry voices, pitched high. But I could not make out the words.

Curiosity got the better of me. If the men were hired by Buell I wanted to know what they were quarrelling about. I stole stealthily from tree to tree, and another hollow opened beneath me. It was so wide and the pines so overshadowed it that I could not tell how close the opposite side might be to the camp-fire. I slipped down along the edge of the trail. The blaze disappeared. Only a faint arc of light showed through the gloom.

I peered keenly into the blackness. At length I reached the slope. Here I dropped to my hands and knees.

It was a long crawl to the top. Reaching it, I cautiously peeped over. There were trees hiding the fire. But it was close. I heard the voices of men. I backed down the slope, crossed the trail, and came up on the other side. Pines grew thick on this level, and I stole silently from one to another. Finally I reached the black trunk of a tree close to the camp-fire.

For a moment I lay low. I did not seem exactly afraid, but I was all tense and hard, and my heart drummed in my ears. There was something ticklish about this scouting. Then I peeped out.

It added little to my excitement to recognize the Mexican. He sat near the fire smoking a cigarette. Near him were several men, one of whom was Bill. Facing them sat a man with his back to a small sapling. He was tied with a lasso.

One glance at his white face made me drop behind the tree, where I lay stunned and bewildered — for that man was Dick Leslie.

73

VIII

The Lumbermen

For a full moment I just lay still, hugging the ground, and I did not seem to think at all. Voices loud in anger roused me. Raising myself, I guardedly looked from behind the tree.

One of the lumbermen threw brush on the fire, making it blaze brightly. He was tall and had a red beard. I recognized Stockton, Buell's right hand in the lumber deal.

"Leslie, you're a liar!" he said.

Dick's eyes glinted from his pale face.

"Yes, that's your speed, Stockton," he retorted. "You bring your thugs into my camp pretending to be friendly. You grab a fellow behind his back, tie him up, and then call him a liar. Wait, you timber shark!"

"You're lying about that kid, Ward," declared the other. "You sent him back East, that's what. He'll have the whole forest service down here. Buell will be wild. Oh, he won't do a thing when he learns Ward has given us the slip!"

"I tell you, Ken Ward gave me the slip." replied Dick. "I'll admit I meant to see him safe in Holston. But he wouldn't go. He ran off from me right here in this forest."

What could have been Dick's object in telling

such a lie? It made me wonder. Perhaps these lumbermen were more dangerous than I had supposed, and Dick did not wish them to believe I had left Penetier. Maybe he was playing for time, and did not want them to get alarmed and escape before the officers came.

"Why did he run off?" asked Stockton.

"Because I meant to send him home, and he didn't want to go. He's crazy to camp out, to hunt and ride."

"If that's true, Leslie, there's been no word sent to Washington."

"How could there be?"

"Well, I've got to hold you anyway till we see Buell. His orders were to keep you and Ward prisoners till this lumber deal is pulled off. We're not going to be stopped now."

Leslie turned crimson, and strained on the lasso that bound him to the sapling.

"Somebody is going to pay for this business!" he declared, savagely. "You forget I'm an officer in this forest."

"I'll hold you, Leslie, whatever comes of it," answered the lumberman. "I'd advise you to cool down."

"You and Buell have barked up the wrong tree, mind that, Stockton. Jim Williams, my pardner, is wise. He expects me back to-morrow."

"See hyar, Stockton," put in Bill, "you're new in Arizona, an' I want to give you a hunch. If Jim Williams hits this trail, you ain't goin' to be well enough to care about any old lumber steal."

75

"Jim'll hit the trail all right," went on Dick. "He's after Greaser. It'd go hard with you if Jim happened to walk in now."

"I don't want to buck against Williams, that's certain," replied Stockton. "I know his record. But I'll take a chance — anyway, till Buell knows. It's his game."

Dick made no answer, and sat there eying his captors. There was little talk after this. Bud threw a log on the fire. Stockton told the Mexican to take a look at the horses. Greaser walked within twenty feet of where I lay, and I held my breath while he passed. The others rolled in their blankets. It was now so dark that I could not distinguish anything outside of the camp-fire circle. But I heard Greaser's soft, shuffling footsteps as he returned. Then his dark, slim figure made a shadow between me and the light. He sat down before the fire and began to roll a cigarette. He did not seem sleepy.

A daring scheme flashed into my mind. I would crawl into camp and free Dick. Not only would I outwit the lumber thieves, but also make Dick think well of me. What would Jim Williams say of a trick like that? The thought of the Texan banished what little hesitation I felt. Glancing round the bright circle, I made my plan; it was to crawl far back into the darkness, go around to the other side of the camp, and then slip up behind Dick. Already his head was nodding on his breast. It made me furious to see him sitting so uncomfortably, sagging in the lasso.

76

I tried to beat down my excitement, but there was a tingling all over me that would not subside. But I soon saw that I might have a long wait. The Mexican did not go to sleep, so I had time to cool off.

The camp-fire gradually burned out, and the white glow changed to red. One of the men snored in a way that sounded like a wheezy whistle. Coyotes howled in the woods, and the longer I listened to the long, strange howls the better I liked them. The roar in the wind had died down to a moaning. I thought of myself lying there, with my skin prickling and my eyes sharp on the darkening forms. I thought of the nights I had spent with Hal in the old woods at home. How full the present seemed! My breast swelled, my hand gripped my revolver, my eyes pierced the darkness, and I would not have been anywhere else for the world.

Greaser smoked out his cigarette, and began to nod. That was the signal for me. I crawled noiselessly from the tree. When I found myself going down into the hollow, I stopped and rose to my feet. The forest was so pitchy black that I could not tell the trees from the darkness. I groped to the left, trying to circle. Once I snapped a twig; it cracked like a pistol-shot, and my heart stopped beating, then began to thump. But Greaser never stirred as he sat in the waning light. At last I had half circled the camp.

After a short rest I started forward, slow and stealthy as a creeping cat. When within fifty feet of the fire I went down on all-fours and began to crawl. Twice I got out of line. But at last Dick's burly shoulders loomed up between me and the light.

Then I halted. My breast seemed bursting, and I panted so hard that I was in a terror lest I should awaken some one. Again I thought of what I was doing, and fought desperately to gain my coolness.

Now the only cover I had was Dick's broad back, for the sapling to which he was tied was small. I drew my hunting-knife.

One more wriggle brought me close to Dick, with my face near his hands, which were bound behind him. I slipped the blade under the lasso, and cut it through.

Dick started as if he had received an electric shock. He threw back his head and uttered a sudden exclamation.

Although I was almost paralyzed with fright I put my hand on his shoulder and whispered: "S-s-s-h! It's Ken!"

Greaser uttered a shrill cry. Dick leaped to his feet. Then I grew dizzy, and my sight blurred. I heard hoarse shouts and saw dark forms rising as if out of the earth. All was confusion. I wanted to run, but could not get up. There was a wrestling, whirling mass in front of me.

But this dimness of sight and weakness of body did not last. I saw two men on the ground, with Dick standing over them. Stockton was closing in. Greaser ran around them with something in his hand that glittered in the firelight. Stockton dived for Dick's legs and upset him. They went down together, and the Mexican leaped on them, waving the bright thing high over his head.

I bounded forward, and, grasping his wrist with both hands, I wrenched his arm with all my might. Some one struck me over the head. I saw a million darting points of light — then all went black.

When I opened my eyes the sun was shining. I had a queer, numb feeling all over, and my head hurt terribly. Everything about me was hazy. I did not know where I was. After a little I struggled to sit up, and with great difficulty managed it. My hands were tied. Then it all came back to me.

Stockton stood before me holding a tin cup of water toward my lips. My throat was parched, and I drank. Stockton had a great bruise on his forehead; his nostrils were crusted with blood, and his shirt was half torn off.

"You're all right?" he said.

"Sure," I replied, which was not true.

I imagined that a look of relief came over his face. Next I saw Bill nursing his eye, and bathing it with a wet handkerchief. It was swollen shut, puffed out to the size of a goose-egg, and blue as indigo. Dick had certainly landed hard on Bill. Then I turned round to see Dick sitting against the little sapling, bound fast with a lasso. His clean face did not look as if he had been in a fight; he was smiling, yet there was anxiety in his eyes.

"Ken, now you've played hob," he said. It was a reproach, but his look made me proud.

"Oh, Dick, if you hadn't called out!" I exclaimed.

"Darned if you're not right! But it was a slick job, and you'll tickle Jim to death. I was an old woman. But that cold knife-blade made me jump."

I glanced round the camp for the Mexican and Bud and the fifth man, but they were gone. Bill varied his occupation of the moment by kneading biscuit dough in a basin. Then there came such a severe pain in my head that I went blind for a little while.

"What's the matter with my head? Who hit me?" I cried.

"Bud slugged you with the butt of his pistol," said Dick. "And, Ken, I think you saved me from being knifed by the Greaser. You twisted his arm half off. He cursed all night. . . . Ha! there he comes now with your outfit."

Sure enough, the Mexican appeared on the trail, leading my horses. I was so glad to see Hal that I forgot I was a prisoner. But Greaser's sullen face and glittering eyes reminded me of it quickly enough. I read treachery in his glance.

Bud rode into camp from the other direction, and he brought a bunch of horses, two of which I recognized as Dick's. The lumbermen set about getting breakfast, and Stockton helped me to what little I could eat and drink. Now that I was caught he did not appear at all mean or harsh. I did not shrink from him, and had the feeling that he meant well by me.

The horses were saddled and bridled, and Dick and I, still tied, were bundled astride our mounts. The pack-ponies led the way, with Bill following; I came next, Greaser rode behind me, and Dick was between Bud and Stockton. So we travelled, and no time was wasted. I noticed that the men kept a sharp lookout both to the fore and the rear. We branched off the main trail and took a steeper one leading up the slope.

We rode for hours. There were moments when I reeled in my saddle, but for the greater while I stood my pain and weariness well enough. Some time in the afternoon a shrill whistle ahead attracted my attention. I made out two horsemen waiting on the trail.

"Huh! about time!" growled Bill. "Hyar's Buell an' Herky-Jerky."

As we approached I saw Buell, and the fellow with the queer name turned out to be no other than the absent man I had been wondering about. He had been dispatched to fetch the lumberman.

Buell was superbly mounted on a sleek bay, and he looked very much the same jovial fellow I had met on the train. He grinned at the disfigured men.

"Take it from me, you fellers wouldn't look any worse bunged up if you'd been jolted by the saw-logs in my mill."

"We can't stand here to crack jokes," said Stockton, sharply. "Some ranger might see us. . . . Now what?"

"You ketched the kid in time. That's all I wanted. Take him an' Leslie up in one of the cañons an' keep them there till further orders. You needn't stay, Stockton, after you get them in a safe place. An' you can send up grub."

Then he turned to me.

"You'll not be hurt if —"

"Don't you speak to me!" I burst out. It was on my lips to tell him of the letter to Washington, but somehow I kept silent.

"Leslie," went on Buell, "I'll overlook your hittin' me an' let you go if you'll give me your word to keep mum about this."

Dick did not speak, but looked at the lumberman with a dark gleam in his eyes.

"There's one thing, Buell," said Stockton. "Jim Williams is wise. You've got to look out for him."

Buell's ruddy face blanched. Then, without another word, he waved his hand toward the slope, and, wheeling his horse, galloped down the trail.

IX

Taken into the Mountains

We climbed to another level bench where we branched off the trail. The forest still kept its open, park-like character. Under the great pines the ground was bare and brown with a thick covering of pine-needles, but in the glades were green grass and blue flowers.

Once across this level we encountered a steeper ascent than any I had yet climbed. Here the character of the forest began to change. There were other trees than pines, and particularly one kind, cone-shaped, symmetrical, and bright, which Dick called a silver spruce. I was glad it belonged to the conifers, or pine-tree family, because it was the most beautiful tree I had ever seen. We climbed ridges and threaded through aspen thickets in hollows till near sunset. Then Stockton ordered a halt for camp.

It came none too soon for me, and I was so exhausted that I had to be helped off my mustang. Stockton arranged my blankets, fed me, and bathed the bruise on my head, but I was too weary and sick to be grateful or to care about anything except sleep. Even the fact that my hands were uncomfortably bound did not keep me awake.

When some one called me next morning my eyes did not want to stay open. I had a lazy feeling and a dull ache in my bones, but the pain had gone from my head. That made everything else seem all right.

Soon we were climbing again, and my interest in my surroundings grew as we went up. For a while we brushed through thickets of scrub-oak. The whole slope of the mountain was ridged and hollowed, so that we were always going down and climbing up. The pines and spruces grew smaller, and were more rugged and gnarled.

"Hyar's the cañon!" sang out Bill, presently.

We came out on the edge of a deep hollow. It was half a mile wide. I looked down a long incline of sharp tree-tips. The roar of water rose from below, and in places a white rushing torrent showed. Above loomed the snow-clad peak, glistening in the morning sun. How wonderfully far off and high it still was!

To my regret it was shut off from my sight as we descended into the cañon. However, I soon forgot that. I saw a troop of coyotes, and many black and white squirrels. From time to time huge birds, almost as big as turkeys, crashed out of the thickets and whirred away. They flew swift as pheasants, and I asked Dick what they were.

"Blue grouse," he replied. "Look sharp now, Ken, there are deer ahead of us. See the tracks?"

Looking down I saw little, sharp-pointed, oval tracks. Presently two foxes crossed an open patch not fifty yards from us, but I did not get a glimpse of the deer. Soon we reached the bottom of the cañon, and struck into another trail. The air was full of the low roar of tumbling water. This mountain-torrent was about twenty feet wide, but its swiftness and foam made it impossible to tell its depth. The trail led upstream, and turned so constantly that half the time Bill, the leader, was not in sight. Once the sharp crack of his rifle halted the train. I heard crashings in the thicket. Dick yelled for me to look up the slope, and there I saw three gray deer with white tails raised. I heard a strange, whistling sound.

On going forward we found that Bill had killed a deer and was roping it on his pack-horse. As we proceeded up the cañon it grew narrower, and soon we entered a veritable gorge. It was short, but the floor was exceedingly rough, and made hard going for the horses. Suddenly I was amazed to see the gorge open out into a kind of amphitheatre several hundred feet across. The walls were steep, and one side shelved out, making a long, shallow cave. In the centre of this amphitheatre was a deep hole from which the mountain stream boiled and bubbled.

"Hyar we are," said Bill, and swung out of his saddle. The other men followed suit, and helped Dick and me down. Stockton untied our hands, saying he reckoned we would be more comfortable that way. Indeed we were. My wrists were swollen and blistered. Stockton detailed the Mexican to keep guard over us.

"Ken, I've heard of this place," said Dick. "How's that for a spring? Twenty yards wide, and no telling how deep! This is snow-water straight from the peaks. We're not a thousand feet below the snow-line."

"I can tell that. Look at those dwarf pines," I replied, pointing up over the wall. A rugged slope rose above our camp-site, and it was covered with a tangled mass of scanted pines. Many of them were twisted and misshapen; some were half dead and bleached white at the tops. "It's my first sight of such trees," I went on, "but I've studied about them. Up here it's not lack of moisture that stunts and retards their growth. It's fighting the elements — cold, storm-winds, snow-slides. I suppose not one in a thousand seedlings takes root and survives. But the forest fights hard to live."

"Well, Ken, we may as well sit back now and talk forestry till Buell skins all he wants of Penetier," said Dick. "It's really a fine camping-spot. Plenty of deer up here — and bear, too."

"Dick, couldn't we escape?" I whispered.

"We're not likely to have a chance. But I say, Ken, how did you happen to turn up? I thought you were going to hop on the first train for home."

"Dick, you had another think coming. I couldn't go home. I'll have a great time yet — I'm having it now."

"Yes, that lump on your head looks like it," replied Dick, with a laugh. "If Bud hadn't put

86

you out we'd have come closer to licking this bunch. Ken, keep your eye on Greaser. He's treacherous. His arm's lame yet."

"We've had two run-ins already," I said. "The third time is the worst, they say. I hope it won't come. . . . But, Dick, I'm as big — I'm bigger than he is."

"Hear the kid talk! I certainly ought to have put you on that train —"

"What train?" asked Stockton, sharply, from our rear. He took us in with suspicious eyes.

"I was telling Ken I ought to have put him on a train for home," answered Dick.

Stockton let the remark pass without further comment; still, he appeared to be doing some hard thinking. He put Dick at one end of the long cave, me at the other. Our bedding was unpacked and placed at our disposal. We made our beds. After that I kept my eyes open and did not miss anything.

"Leslie, I'm going to treat you and Ward white," said Stockton. "You'll have good grub. Herky-Jerky's the best cook this side of Holston, and you'll be left untied in the daytime. But if either of you attempts to get away it means a leg shot off. Do you get that?"

"All right, Stockton; that's pretty square of you, considering," replied Dick. "You're a decent sort of chap to be mixed up with a thief like Buell. I'm sorry."

Stockton turned away at this rather abruptly. Then Bill appeared on the wall above, and began to throw down fire-wood. Bud returned from the cañon, where he had driven the horses. Greaser sat on a stone puffing a cigarette. It was the first time I had taken a good look at him. He was smaller than I had fancied; his feet and hands and features resembled those of a woman, but his eyes were live coals of black fire. In the daylight I was not in the least afraid of him.

Herky-Jerky was the most interesting one of our captors. He had a short, stocky figure, and was the most bow-legged man I ever saw. Never on earth could he have stopped a pig in a lane. A stubby beard covered the lower half of his brick-red face. The most striking thing about Herky-Jerky, however, was his perpetual grin. He looked very jolly, yet every time he opened his mouth it was to utter bad language. He cursed the fire, the pans, the coffee, the biscuits, all of which he handled most skilfully. It was disgusting, and yet aside from this I rather liked him.

It grew dark very quickly while we were eating, and the wind that dipped down into the gorge was cold. I kept edging closer and closer to the blazing camp-fire. I had never tasted venison before, and rather disliked it at first. But I soon cultivated a liking for it.

That night Stockton tied me securely, but in a way which made it easy for me to turn. I slept soundly and awoke late. When I sat up Stockton stood by his saddled horse, and was giving orders to the men. He spoke sharply. He made it clear that they were not to be lax in their vigilance. Then, without a word to Dick or me, he rode down the gorge and disappeared behind a corner of yellow wall.

Bill untied the rope that held Dick's arms, but left his feet bound. I was freed entirely, and it felt so good to have the use of all my limbs once more that I pranced round in a rather lively way. Either my antics annoyed Herky-Jerky or he thought it a good opportunity to show his skill with a lasso, for he shot the loop over me so hard that it stung my back.

"I'm all there as a roper!" he said, pulling the lasso tight round my middle. The men all laughed as I tumbled over in the gravel.

"Better keep a half-hitch on the colt," remarked Bud.

So they left the lasso fast about my waist, and it trailed after me as I walked. Herky-Jerky put me to carrying Dick's breakfast from the camp-fire up into the cave. This I did with alacrity. Dick and I exchanged commonplace remarks aloud, but we had several little whispers.

"Ken, we may get the drop on them or give them the slip yet," whispered Dick, in one of these interludes.

This put ideas into my head. There might be a chance for me to escape, if not for Dick. I made up my mind to try if a good chance offered, but I did not want to go alone down that cañon without a gun. Stockton had taken my revolver and hunting-knife, but I still had the little leather case which Hal and I had used so often back on the Susquehanna. Besides a pen-knife this case contained salt and pepper, fishing hooks and lines, matches — a host of little things that a boy who had never been lost might imagine he would need in an emergency. While thinking and planning I sat on the edge of the great hole where the spring was. Suddenly I saw a swirl in the water, and then a splendid spotted fish. It broke water twice. It was two feet long.

"Dick, there's fish in this hole!" I yelled, eagerly.

"Shouldn't wonder," replied he.

"Sure, kid, thet hole's full of trout — speckled trout," said Herky-Jerky. "But they can't be ketched."

"Why not?" I demanded. I had not caught little trout in the Pennsylvania hills for nothing. "They eat, don't they? That fish I saw was a whale, and he broke water for a bug. Get me a pole and some bugs or worms!"

When I took out my little case and showed the fishing-line, Herky-Jerky said he would find me some bait.

While he was absent I studied that spring with new and awakened eyes. It was round and very deep, and the water bulged up in great greenish swirls. The outlet was a narrow little cleft through which the water flowed slowly, as though it did not want to take its freedom. The rush and roar came from the gorge below.

Herky-Jerky returned with a long, slender

pole. It was as pliant as a buggy-whip, and once trimmed and rigged it was far from being a poor tackle. Herky-Jerky watched me with extreme attention, all the time grinning. Then he held out a handful of grubs.

"If you ketch a trout on thet I'll swaller the pole!" he exclaimed.

I stooped low and approached the spring, being careful to keep out of sight.

"You forgot to spit on yer bait, kid," said Bill.

They all laughed in a way to rouse my ire. But despite it I flipped the bait into the water with the same old thrilling expectancy.

The bait dropped with a little spat. An arrowy shadow, black and gold, flashed up. Splash! The line hissed. Then I jerked hard. The pole bent double, wobbled, and swayed this way and that. The fish was a powerful one; his rushes were like those of a heavy bass. But never had a bass given me such a struggle. Every instant I made sure the tackle would be wrecked. Then, just at the breaking-point, the fish would turn. At last he began to tire. I felt that he was rising to the surface, and I put on more strain. Soon I saw him; then he turned, flashing like a gold bar. I led my captive to the outlet of the spring, where I reached down and got my fingers in his gills. With that I lifted him. Dick whooped when I held up the fish; as for me, I was speechless. The trout was almost two feet long, broad and heavy, with shiny sides flecked with color.

Herky-Jerky celebrated my luck with a generous outburst of enthusiasm, whereupon his comrades reminded him of his offer to swallow my fishing-pole.

I put on a fresh bait and instantly hooked another fish, a smaller one, which was not so hard to land. The spring hole was full of trout. They made the water boil when I cast. Several large ones tore the hook loose; I had never dreamed of such fishing. Really it was a strange situation. Here I was a prisoner, with Greaser or Bud taking turns at holding the other end of the lasso. More than once they tethered me up short for no other reason than to torment me. Yet never in my life had I so enjoyed fishing.

By-and-by Bill and Herky-Jerky left the camp. I heard Herky tell Greaser to keep his eye on the stew-pots, and it occurred to me that Greaser had better keep his eye on Ken Ward. When I saw Bud lie down I remembered what Dick had whispered. I pretended to be absorbed in my fishing, but really I was watching Greaser. As usual, he was smoking, and appeared listless, but he still held on to the lasso.

Suddenly I saw a big blue revolver lying on a stone, and I could even catch the glint of brass shells in the cylinder. It was not close to Bud nor so very close to Greaser. If he should drop the lasso! A wild idea possessed me — held me in its grip.

Just then the stew-pot boiled over. There was a sputter and a cloud of steam. Greaser lazily swore in Mexican; he got up to move the stew-pot and dropped the lasso.

When he reached the fire I bounded up, jerking the lasso far behind me. I ran and grabbed the revolver. Greaser heard me and wheeled with a yell. Bud sat up quickly. I pointed the revolver at him, then at Greaser, and kept moving it from one side to the other.

"Don't move! I'll shoot!" I cried.

"Good boy!" yelled Dick. "You've got the drop. Keep it, Ken, keep it! Don't lose your nerve. Edge round here and cut me loose. . . . Bud, if you move I'll make him shoot. Come on, Ken."

"Greaser, cut him loose!" I commanded the snarling Mexican.

I trembled so that the revolver wabbled in my hand. Trying to hold it steadier, I squeezed it hard. Bang! It went off with a bellow like a cannon. The bullet scattered the gravel near Greaser. His yellow face turned a dirty white. He jumped straight up in his fright.

"Cut him loose!" I ordered.

Greaser ran toward Dick.

"Look out, Ken! Behind you! Quick!" yelled Dick.

I heard a crunching of gravel. Even as I wheeled I felt a tremendous pull on the lasso and I seemed to be sailing in the air. I got a blurred glimpse of Herky-Jerky leaning back on the taut lasso. Then I plunged down, slid over the rocks, and went souse into the spring.

X

Escape

Down, down I plunged, and the shock of the icy water seemed to petrify me. I should have gone straight to the bottom like a piece of lead but for the lasso. It tightened around my chest, and began to haul me up.

I felt the air and the light, and opened my eyes to see Herky-Jerky hauling away on the rope. When he caught sight of me he looked as if ready to dodge behind the bank.

"Whar's my gun?" he yelled.

I had dropped it in the spring. He let the lasso sag, and I had to swim. Then, seeing that my hands were empty, he began to swear and to drag me round and round in the pool. When he had pulled me across he ran to the other side and jerked me back. I was drawn through the water with a force that I feared would tear me apart. Greaser chattered like a hideous monkey, and ran to and fro in glee. Herky-Jerky soon had me sputtering, gasping, choking. When he finally pulled me out of the hole I was all but drowned.

"You bow-legged beggar!" shouted Dick, "I'll fix you for that."

"Whar's my gun?" yelled Herky, as I fell to the ground.

"I — lost — it," I panted.

He began to rave. Then I half swooned, and when sight and hearing fully returned I was lying in the cave on my blankets. A great lassitude weighted me down. The terrible thrashing about in the icy water had quenched my spirit. For a while I was too played out to move, and lay there in my wet clothes. Finally I asked leave to take them off. Bud, who had come back in the mean time, helped me, or I should never have got out of them. Herky brought up my coat, which, fortunately, I had taken off before the ducking. I did not have the heart to speak to Dick or look at him, so I closed my eyes and fell asleep.

It was another day when I awoke. I felt all right except for a soreness under my arms and across my chest where the lasso had chafed and bruised me. Still I did not recover my good spirits. Herky-Jerky kept on grinning and cracking jokes on my failure to escape. He had appropriated my revolver for himself, and he asked me several times if I wanted to borrow it to shoot Greaser.

That day passed quietly, and so did the two that followed. The men would not let me fish nor move about. They had been expecting Stockton, and as he did not come it was decided to send Bud down to the mill; in fact, Bud decided the matter himself. He warned Greaser and Herky to keep close watch over Dick and me. Then he rode away. Dick and I resumed our talk about forestry, and as we were separated by the length of the cave it was necessary to speak loud. So our captors heard every word we said.

"Ken, what's the difference between Government forestry out here and, say, forestry practised by a farmer back in Pennsylvania?" asked Dick.

"There's a big difference, I imagine. Forestry is established in some parts of the East; it's only an experiment out here."

Then I went on to tell him about the method of the farmer. He usually had a small piece of forest, mostly hard wood. When the snow was on he cut fire-wood, fence-rails, and lumber for his own use in building. Some seasons lumber brought high prices; then he would select matured logs and haul them to the sawmill. But he would not cut a great deal, and he would use care in the selection. It was his aim to keep the land well covered with forest. He would sow as well as harvest.

"Now the Government policy is to preserve the National Forests for the use of the people. The soil must be kept productive. Agriculture would be impossible without water, and the forests hold water. The West wants people to come to stay. The lumberman who slashes off the timber may get rich himself, but he ruins the land."

"What's that new law Congress is trying to pass?" queried Dick.

I was puzzled, but presently I caught his

meaning. Bill and Herky-Jerky were hanging on our words with unconcealed attention. Even the Mexican was listening. Dick's cue was to scare them, or at least to have some fun at their expense.

"They've passed it," I replied. "Fellows like Buell will go to the penitentiary for life. His men'll get twenty years on bread and water. No whiskey! Serves 'em right."

"What'll the President do when he learns these men kidnapped you?"

"Do? He'll have the whole forest service out here and the National Guard. He's a friend of my father's. Why, these kidnappers will be hanged!"

"I wish the Guard would come quick. Too bad you couldn't have sent word! I'd enjoy seeing Greaser swing. Say, he hasn't a ghost of a chance, with the President and Jim Williams after him."

"Dick, I want the rings in Greaser's ears."

"What for? They're only brass."

"Souvenirs. Maybe I'll have watch-charms made of them. Anyway, I can show them to my friends back East."

"It'll be great — what you'll have to tell," went on Dick. "It'll be funny, too."

Greaser had begun to snarl viciously, and Herky and Bill looked glum and thoughtful. The arrival of Bud interrupted the conversation and put an end to our playful mood. We heard a little of what he told his comrades, and gathered that Jim Williams had met Stockton and had asked questions hard to answer. Dick flashed me a significant look, which was as much as to say that Jim was growing suspicious. Bud had brought a store of whiskey, and his companions now kept closer company with him than ever before. But from appearances they did not get all they wanted.

"We've got to move this here camp," said Bud.

Bud and Bill and Herky walked off down the gorge. Perhaps they really went to find another place for the camp, for the present spot was certainly a kind of trap. But from the looks of Greaser I guessed that they were leaving him to keep guard while they went off to drink by themselves. Greaser muttered and snarled. As the moments passed his face grew sullen.

All at once he came toward me. He bound my hands and my feet. Dick was already securely tied, but Greaser put another lasso on him. Then he slouched down the gorge. His high-peaked Mexican sombrero bobbed above the rocks, then disappeared.

"Ken, now's the chance," said Dick, low and quick. "If you can only work loose! There's your rifle and mine, too. We could hold this fort for a month."

"What can I do?" I asked straining on my ropes.

"You're not fast to the rock, as I am. Roll over here and untie me with your teeth."

98

I raised my head to get the direction, and then, with a violent twist of my body, I started toward him; but being bound fast I could not guide myself, and I rolled off the ledge. The bank there was pretty steep, and, unable to stop, I kept on like a barrel going down-hill. The thought of rolling into the spring filled me with horror. Suddenly I bumped hard into something that checked me. It was a log of fire-wood, and in one end stuck the big knife which Herky-Jerky used to cut meat.

Instantly I conceived the idea of cutting my bonds with this knife. But how was I to set about it?

"Dick, here's a knife. How'll I get to it so as to free myself?"

"Easy as pie," replied he, eagerly. "The sharp edge points down. You hitch yourself this way — That's it — good!"

What Dick called easy as pie was the hardest work I ever did. I lay flat on my back, bound hand and foot, and it was necessary to jerk my body along the log till my hands should be under the knife. I lifted my legs and edged along inch by inch.

"Fine work, Ken! Now you're right! Turn on your side! Be careful you don't loosen the knife!"

Not only were my wrists bound, but the lasso had been wrapped round my elbows, holding them close to my body. Turning on my side, I found that I could not reach the knife — not by several inches. This was a bitter disappointment.

I strained and heaved. In my effort to lift my body sidewise I pressed my face into the gravel.

"Hurry, Ken, hurry!" cried Dick. "Somebody's coming!"

Thus urged, I grew desperate. In my struggle I discovered that it was possible to edge up on the log and stick there. I glued myself to that log. By dint of great exertion I brought the tight cord against the blade. It parted with a little snap, my elbows dropped free. Raising my wrists, I sawed quickly through the bonds. I cut myself, the blood flowed, but that was no matter. Jerking the knife from the log, I severed the ropes round my ankles and leaped up.

"Hurry, boy!" cried Dick, with a sharp note of alarm.

I ran to where he lay, and attacked the heavy halter with which he had been secured. I had cut half through the knots when a shrill cry arrested me. It was the Mexican's voice.

"Head him off! He's after your gun!" yelled Dick.

The sight of Greaser running toward the cave put me into a frenzy. Dropping the knife, I darted to where my rifle leaned across my saddle. But I saw the Mexican would beat me to it. Checking my speed, I grabbed up a round stone and let fly. That was where my ball-playing stood me in good stead, for the stone hit Greaser on the shoulder, knocking him flat. But he got up, and lunged for the rifle just as I reached him.

I kicked the rifle out of his hand, grappled with him, and down we went together. We wrestled and thrashed off the ledge, and when we landed in the gravel I was on top.

"Slug him, Ken!" yelled Dick, wildly. "Oh, that's fine! Give it to him! Punch him! Get his wind!"

Either it was a mortal dread of Greaser's knife or some kind of a new-born fury that lent me such strength. He screeched, he snapped like a wolf, he clawed me, he struck me, but he could not shake me off. Several times he had me turning, but a hard rap on his head knocked him back again. Then I began to bang him in the ribs.

"That's the place!" shouted Dick. "Ken, you're going to do him up! Soak him! Oh-h, but this is great!"

I kept the advantage over Greaser, but still he punished me cruelly. Suddenly he got his snaky hands on my throat and began to choke me. With all my might I swung my fist into his stomach.

His hands dropped, his mouth opened in a gasp, his face turned green. The blow had made him horribly sick, and he sank back utterly helpless. I jumped up with a shout of triumph.

"Run! Run for it!" yelled Dick, in piercing tones. "They're coming! Never mind me! *Run,* I tell you! Not down the gorge! Climb out!"

For a moment I could not move out of my tracks. Then I saw Bill and Herky running up the gorge, and, farther down, Bud staggering and lurching.

This lent me wings. In two jumps I had grabbed my rifle; then, turning, I ran round the pool, and started up the one place in the steep wall where climbing was possible. Above the yells of the men I heard Dick's piercing cry:

"Go — go — go, Ken!"

I sent the loose rocks down in my flight. Here I leaped up; there I ran along a little ledge; in another place I climbed hand and foot. The last few yards was a gravelly incline. I seemed to slide back as much as I gained.

"Come back hyar!" bawled Bill.

Crack! Crack! Crack! The reports rang out in quick succession. A bullet whistled over me, another struck the gravel and sent a shower of dust into my face. I pitched my rifle up over the bank and began to dig my fingers and toes into the loose ground. As I gained the top two more bullets sang past my head so close that I knew Bill was aiming to more than scare me. I dragged myself over the edge and was safe.

The cañon, with its dense thickets and scrubby clumps of trees, lay below in plain sight. Once hidden there, I would be hard to find. Picking up my rifle, I ran swiftly along the base of the slope and soon gained the cover of the woods.

XI

The Old Hunter

I ran till I got a stitch in my side, and then slowed down to a dog-trot. The one thing to do was to get a long way ahead of my pursuers, for surely at the outset they would stick like hounds to my trail.

A mile or more below the gorge I took to the stream and waded. It was slippery, dangerous work, for the current tore about my legs and threatened to upset me. After a little I crossed to the left bank. Here the slope of the cañon was thick with grass that hid my tracks. It was a long climb up to the level. Upon reaching it I dropped, exhausted.

"I've — given them — the slip," I panted, exultantly . . . "But — now what?"

It struck me that now I was free I had only jumped out of the frying-pan into the fire. Hurriedly I examined my Winchester. The magazine contained ten cartridges. What luck that Stockton had neglected to unload it! This made things look better. I had salt and pepper, a knife, and matches — thanks to the little leather case — and so I could live in the woods.

It was too late for regrets. I might have freed Dick somehow or even held the men at bay, but

103

I had thought only of escape. The lack of nerve and judgment stung me. Then I was bitter over losing my mustang and outfit.

But on thinking it all over, I concluded that I ought to be thankful for things as they were. I was free, with a whole skin. That climb out of the gorge had been no small risk. How those bullets had whistled and hissed!

"I'm pretty lucky," I muttered. "Now to get good and clear of this vicinity. They'll ride down the trail after me. Better go over this ridge into the next cañon and strike down that. I must go down. But how far? What must I strike for?"

I took a long look at the cañon. In places the stream showed, also the trail; then there were open patches, but I saw no horses or men. With a grim certainty that I should be lost in a very little while, I turned into the cool, dark forest.

Every stone and log, every bit of hard ground in my path, served to help hide my trail. Herky-Jerky very likely had the cowboy's skill at finding tracks, but I left few traces of my presence on that long slope. Only an Indian or a hound could have trailed me. The timber was small and rough, brush grew everywhere. Presently I saw light ahead, and I came to an open space. It was a wide swath in the forest. At once I recognized the path of an avalanche. It sloped up clean and bare to the gray cliffs far above. Below was a great mass of trees and rocks, all tangled in black splintered ruin.

I pushed on across the path, into the forest,

and up and down the hollows. The sun had gone down behind the mountain, and the shadows were gathering when I came to another large cañon. It looked so much like the first that I feared I had been travelling in a circle. But this one seemed wider, deeper, and there was no roar of rushing water.

It was time to think of making camp, and so I hurried down the slope. At the bottom I found a small brook winding among bowlders and ledges of rock. The far side of this cañon was steep and craggy. Soon I discovered a place where I thought it would be safe to build a fire. My clothes were wet, and the air had grown keen and cold. Gathering a store of wood, I made my fire in a niche. For a bed I cut some sweet-scented pine boughs (I thought they must be from a balsam-tree), and these I laid close up in a rocky corner. Thus I had the fire between me and the opening, and with plenty of wood to burn I did not fear visits from bears or lions. At last I lay down, dry and warm indeed, but very tired and hungry.

Darkness closed in upon me. I saw a few stars, heard the cheery crackle of my fire, and then I fell asleep. Twice in the night I awakened cold, but by putting on more fire-wood I was soon comfortable again.

When I awoke the sun was shining brightly into my rocky bedchamber. The fire had died out completely, there was frost on the stones. To build up another fire and to bathe my face in the ice-water of the brook were my first tasks. The air was sweet; it seemed to freeze as I breathed, and was a bracing tonic. I was tingling all over, and as hungry as a starved wolf.

I set forth on a hunt for game. Even if the sound of a shot betrayed my whereabouts I should have to abide by it, for I had to eat. Stepping softly along, I glanced about me with sharp eyes. Deer trails were thick. The bottom of this cañon was very wide, and grew wider as I proceeded. Then the pines once more became large and thrifty. I judged I had come down the mountain, perhaps a couple of thousand feet below the camp in the gorge. I flushed many of the big blue grouse, and I saw numerous coyotes, a fox, and a large brown beast which moved swiftly into a thicket. It was enough to make my heart rise in my throat. To dream of hunting bears was something vastly different from meeting one in a lonely cañon.

Just after this I saw a herd of deer. They were a good way off. I began to slip from tree to tree, and drew closer. Presently I came to a little hollow with a thick, short patch of underbrush growing on the opposite side. Something crashed in the thicket. Then two beautiful deer ran out. One bounded leisurely up the slope; the other, with long ears erect, stopped to look at me. It was not more than fifty yards away. Trembling with eagerness, I levelled my rifle. I could not get the sight to stay steady on the deer. Even then, with the rifle wobbling in my intense excitement, I thought of how beautiful that wild creature was. Straining every nerve, I drew the sight till it was in line with the gray shape, then fired. The deer leaped down the slope, staggered, and crumpled down in a heap.

I tore through the bushes, and had almost reached the bottom of the hollow when I remembered that a wounded deer was dangerous. So I halted. The gray form was as still as stone. I ventured closer. The deer was dead. My bullet had entered high above the shoulder at the juncture of the neck. Though I had only aimed at him generally, I took a good deal of pride in my first shot at a deer.

Fortunately my pen-knife had a fair-size blade. With it I decided to cut out part of the deer and carry it back to my camp. Then it occurred to me that I might as well camp where I was. There were several jumbles of rock and a cliff within a stone's-throw of where I stood. Besides, I must get used to making camp wherever I happened to be. Accordingly, I took hold of the deer, and dragged him down the hollow till I came to a leaning slab of rock.

Skinning a deer was, of course, new to me. I haggled the flesh somewhat and cut through the skin often, my knife-blade being much too small for such work. Finally I thought it would be enough for me to cut out the haunches, and then I got down to one haunch. It had bothered me how I was going to sever the joint, but to my great surprise I found there did not seem to be any connection between the bones. The haunch came out easily, and I hung it up on a branch while making a fire.

Herky-Jerky's method of broiling a piece of venison at the end of a stick solved the problem of cooking. Then it was that the little flat flask, full of mixed salt and pepper, rewarded me for the long carrying of it. I was hungry, and I feasted.

By this time the sun shone warm, and the cañon was delightful. I roamed around, sat on sunny stones, and lay in the shade of pines. Deer browsed in the glades. When they winded or saw me they would stand erect, shoot up their long ears, and then leisurely lope away. Coyotes trotted out of thickets and watched me suspiciously. I could have shot several, but deemed it wise to be saving of my ammunition. Once I heard a low drumming. I could not imagine what made it. Then a big blue grouse strutted out of a patch of bushes. He spread his wings and tail and neck feathers, after the fashion of a turkey-gobbler. It was a flap or shake of his wings that produced the drumming. I wondered if he intended, by his actions, to frighten me away from his mate's nest. So I went toward him, and got very close before he flew. I caught sight of his mate in the bushes, and, as I had supposed, she was on a nest. Though wanting to see her eggs or young ones, I resisted the temptation, for I was afraid if I went nearer she might abandon her nest, as some mother birds do.

It did not seem to me that I was lost, yet lost I was. The peaks were not in sight. The cañon widened down the slope, and I was pretty sure that it opened out flat into the great pine forest of Penetier. The only thing that bothered me was the loss of my mustang and outfit; I could not reconcile myself to that. So I wandered about with a strange, full sense of freedom such as I had never before known. What was to be the end of my adventure I could not guess, and I wasted no time worrying over it.

The knowledge I had of forestry I tried to apply. I studied the north and south slopes of the cañon, observing how the trees prospered on the sunny side. Certain saplings of a species unknown to me had been gnawed fully ten feet from the ground. This puzzled me. Squirrels could not have done it, nor rabbits, nor birds. Presently I hit upon the solution. The bark and boughs of this particular sapling were food for deer, and to gnaw so high the deer must have stood upon six or seven feet of snow.

I dug into the soft duff under the pines. This covering of the roots was very thick and deep. I made it out to be composed of pine-needles, leaves, and earth. It was like a sponge. No wonder such covering held the water! I pried bark off dead trees and dug into decayed logs to find the insect enemies of the trees. The open places, where little colonies of pine sprouts grew, seemed generally to be down-slope from the parent trees. It was easy to tell the places where the wind had blown the seeds.

The hours sped by. The shadows of the pines lengthened, the sun set, and the shade deepened in the hollows. Returning to my camp, I cooked my supper and made my bed. When I had laid up a store of fire-wood it was nearly dark.

With night came the coyotes. The carcass of the deer attracted them, and they approached from all directions. At first it was fascinating to hear one howl far off in the forest, and then to notice the difference in the sound as he came nearer and nearer. The way they barked and snapped out there in the darkness was as wild a thing to hear as any boy could have wished for. It began to be a little too much for me. I kept up a bright fire, and, though not exactly afraid, I had a perch picked out in the nearest tree.

Suddenly the coyotes became silent. Then a low, continuous growling, a snapping of twigs, and the unmistakable drag of a heavy body over the ground made my hair stand on end. Gripping my rifle, I listened. I heard the crunch of teeth on bones, then more sounds of something being dragged down the hollow. The coyotes began to bark again, but now far back in the forest.

Some beast had frightened them. What was it? I did not know whether a bear would eat deer flesh, but I thought not. Perhaps timber-wolves had disturbed the coyotes. But would they run from wolves? It came to me suddenly — a mountain-lion!

I hugged my fire, and sat there, listening with all my ears, imagining every rustle of leaf to be the step of a lion. It was long before the thrills and shivers stopped chasing over me, longer before I could decide to lie down. But after a while the dead quiet of the forest persuaded me that the night was far advanced, and I fell asleep.

The first thing in the morning I took my rifle and went out to where I had left the carcass of the deer. It was gone. It had been dragged away. A dark path on the pine-needles and grass, and small bushes pressed to the ground, plainly marked the trail. But search as I might, I could not find the track of the animal that had dragged off the deer. After following the trail for a few rods, I decided to return to camp and cook breakfast before going any farther. While I was at it I cut many thin slices of venison, and, after roasting them, I stored them away in the capacious pocket of my coat.

My breakfast finished, I again set out to see what had become of the remains of the deer. In two or three places the sharp hoofs had cut lines in the soft earth, and there were tufts of whitish-gray hair elsewhere. A hundred yards or more down the hollow I came to a bare spot where recently there had been a pool of water. Here I found cat tracks as large as my two hands. I had never seen the track of a mountain-lion, but, all the same, I knew that this was the real thing. What an enormous brute he must have been! I cast fearful glances into the surrounding thickets.

It was not needful to travel much farther. Under a bush well hidden in a clump of trees lay what now remained of my deer. A patch of gray hair, a few long bones, a split skull, and two longs ears — no more! Even the hide was gone. Perhaps the coyotes had finished the job after the lion had gorged himself, but I did not think so. It seemed to me that coyotes would have scattered the remains. Those two long ears somehow seemed pathetic. I wished for a second that the lion were in range of my rifle.

The lion was driven from my mind when I saw a troop of deer cross a glade below me. I had to fight myself to keep from shooting. The wind blew rather strong in my face, which probably accounted for the deer not winding me.

Then the whip-like crack of a rifle riveted me where I stood. One of the deer fell, and the others bounded away. I saw a tall man stride down the slope and into the glade. He was not like any of the loggers or lumbermen. They were mostly brawny and round-shouldered. This man was lithe, erect; he walked like athletes I had seen. Surely I should find a friend in him, and I lost no time in running down into the glade. He saw me as soon as I was clear of the trees, and stood leaning on his rifle.

"Wal, dog-gone my buttons!" he ejaculated. "Who're you?"

I blurted out all about myself, at the same time taking stock of him. He was not young, but I had never seen a young man so splendid. Hair, beard, and skin were all of a dark gray. His eyes, too, were gray — the keenest and clearest I had ever looked into. They shone with a kindly light, otherwise I might have thought his face hard and stern. His shoulders were very wide, his arms long, his hands enormous. His buckskin shirt attracted my attention to his other clothes, which looked like leather overalls or heavy canvas. A belt carried a huge knife and a number of shells of large calibre; the Winchester he had was exceedingly long and heavy, and of an old pattern. The look of him brought back my old fancy of Wetzel or Kit Carson.

"So I'm lost," I concluded, "and don't know what to do. I daren't try to find the sawmill. I won't go back to Holston just yet."

"An' why not, youngster? 'Pears to me you'd better make tracks from Penetier."

I told him why, at which he laughed.

"Wal, I reckon you can stay with me fer a spell. My camp's in the head of this cañon."

"Oh, thank you, that'll be fine!" I exclaimed. My great good luck filled me with joy. "Do you stay on the mountain?"

"Be'n here goin' on eighteen years, youngster. Mebbe you've heerd my name. Hiram Bent."

"Are you a hunter?"

"Wal, I reckon so, though I'm more a trapper. Here, you pack my gun."

With that he drew his knife and set to work on the deer. It was wonderful to see his skill. In a few cuts and strokes, a ripping of the hide and a powerful slash, he had cut out a haunch. It took even less work for the second. Then he hung the rest of the deer on a snag, and wiped his knife and hands on the grass.

"Come on, youngster," he said, starting up the cañon.

I showed him where the carcass of my deer had been devoured.

"Cougar. Thar's a big feller has the run of this cañon."

"Cougar? I thought it was a mountain-lion."

"Cougar, painter, panther, lion — all the same critter. An' if you leave him alone he'll not bother you, but he's bad in a corner."

"He scared away the coyotes."

"Youngster, even a silver-tip — thet's a grizzly bear — will make tracks away from a cougar. I lent my pack of hounds to a pard over near Springer. If I had them we'd put thet cougar up a tree in no time."

"Are there many lions — cougars here?"

"On'y a few. Thet's why there's plenty of deer. Other game is plentiful, too. Foxes, wolves, an', up in the mountains, bears are thick."

"Then I may get to see one — get a shot at one?"

"Wal, I reckon."

From that time I trod on air. I found myself wishing for my brother Hal. I became reconciled to the loss of mustang and outfit. For a moment I almost forgot Dick and Buell. Forestry seemed less important than hunting. I had read a thousand books about old hunters and trappers, and here I was in a wild mountain cañon with a hunter who might have stepped out of one of my dreams.

So I trudged along beside him, asking a question now and then, and listening always. He certainly knew what would interest me. There was scarcely a thing he said that I would ever forget. After a while, however, the trail became so steep and rough that I, at least, had no breath to spare for talking. We climbed and climbed. The cañon had become a narrow, rocky cleft. Huge stones blocked the way. A ragged growth of underbrush fringed the stream. Dead pines, with branches like spears, lay along the trail.

We came upon a little clearing, where there was a rude log-cabin with a stone chimney. Skins of animals were tacked upon logs. Under the bank was a spring. The mountain overshadowed this wild nook.

"Wal, youngster, here's my shack. Make yourself to home," said Hiram Bent.

I was all eyes as we entered the cabin. Skins, large and small, and of many colors, hung upon the walls. A fire burned in a wide stone grate. A rough table and some pans and cooking utensils showed evidence of recent scouring. A bunch of steel traps lay in a corner. Upon a shelf were tin cans and cloth bags, and against the wall stood a bed of glossy bearskins. To me the cabin was altogether a most satisfactory place.

"I reckon ye're tired?" asked the hunter.

"Thet's some pumpkins of a climb unless you're used to it."

I admitted I was pretty tired.

"Wal, rest awhile. You look like you hadn't slept much."

He asked me about my people and home, and was so interested in forestry that he left off his task of the moment to talk about it. I was not long in discovering that what he did not know about trees and forests was hardly worth learning. He called it plain woodcraft. He had never heard of forestry. All the same I hungered for his knowledge. How lucky for me to fall in with him! The things that had puzzled me about the pines he answered easily. Then he volunteered information. From talking of the forest, he drifted to the lumbermen.

"Wal, the lumber-sharks are rippin' holes in Penetier. I reckon they wouldn't stop at nothin'. I've heered some tough stories about thet saw-mill gang. I ain't acquainted with Leslie, or any of them fellers you named except Jim Williams. I knowed Jim. He was in Springer fer a while. If Jim's your friend, there'll be somethin' happening, when he rounds up them kidnappers. I reckon you'd better hang up with me fer a while. You don't want to get ketched again. Your life wasn't much to them fellers. I think they'd held on to you fer money. It's too bad you didn't send word home to your people."

"I sent word home about the big steal of timber. That was before I got kidnapped. By this

116

time the Government knows."

"Wal, you don't say! Thet was pert of you, youngster. An' will the Government round up these sharks?"

"Indeed it will. The Government is in dead earnest about protecting the National Forests."

"So it ought to be. Next to a forest fire, I hate these skinned timber tracts. Wal, old Penetier's going to see somethin' lively before long. Youngster, them lumbermen — leastways, them fellers you call Bud an' Bill, an' such — they're goin' to fight."

The old hunter left me presently, and went outside. I waited awhile for him, but as he did not return I lay down upon the bearskins and dropped to sleep. It seemed I had hardly closed my eyes when I felt a hand on my arm and heard a voice.

"Wake up, youngster. Thar's two old bears an' a cub been foolin' with one of my traps."

In a flash I was wide awake.

"Let's see your gun. Humph! pretty small — .38 caliber, ain't it? Wal, it'll do the work if you hold straight. Can you shoot?"

"Fairly well."

He took his heavy Winchester, and threw a coil of thin rope over his shoulder.

"Come on. Stay close to me, an' keep your eyes peeled."

XII

Bears

The old hunter walked so swiftly that I had to run to keep up with him. The trail led up the creek, now on one side, again on the other, and I was constantly skipping from stone to stone. The grassy slopes grew fewer, and finally gave way altogether to cracked cliffs and weathered rocks. A fringe of pine-trees leaned over the top with here and there a blasted spear standing out white.

"I had my trap set up thet draw," said Hiram Bent, as he pointed toward an intersecting cañon. "Just before I waked you I was comin' along here, an' I heered an all-fired racket up thar, an' so I watched. Soon three black bears come paddlin' down, an' the biggest was draggin' the trap with the chain an' log. Then I hurried to tell you. They can't be far."

"Are they grizzlies?" I asked, trying to speak naturally.

"Nope. Jest plain black bears. But the one with the trap is a whopper. He'll go over four hundred. See the tracks? Looks like somebody'd been plowin' up the stones."

There were deep tracks in the sand, and broad furrows, and stones overturned, and places where a heavy object had crushed the gravel even and smooth.

The old hunter kept striding on, and I wondered how he could go so fast without running. Presently we came to where the cañon forked. Hiram started up the right-hand fork, then suddenly stopped, and, turning, began to go back, carefully examining the ground.

"They've split on us," he explained. "The ole feller with the trap went up the right-hand draw, an' the mother an' cub took to the left. . . . Now, youngster, can you keep your nerve?"

"I think so."

"Wal, you go after the ole feller. You can't miss him, an' he won't be far. You'll hear him bellerin' long before you git to him, though he might lay low, so you steer clear of big bowlders an' thickets. Kill him, an' then run back an' take up this draw. The she bear is cute an' may give me the slip, but if she doesn't climb out soon I'll head her off. Hurry on, now. Keep your eye peeled, an' you'll be safe as if you were to home."

With that he disappeared round the corner of stone wall where the cañon divided.

I wheeled and went to the right. This wing of the cañon twisted and turned and was full of stones. A shallow sheet of water gleamed over its colored bed of gravel. The walls were straight up, and, in places, bulged outward. I flinched at every turn in the cañon; but, with rifle cocked and thrust forward, I went on. The cracks in the walls, the bowlders and pieces of cliff that obstructed my path, and the occasional thickets — all made me halt with careful step and finger on the trigger. I followed the splashes on the stones, which told me that the bear had passed that way. As I went cautiously on I felt a tightening at my throat. The light above grew dimmer. When I stopped to listen it was so silent that I heard only the pounding of my heart and my own quick breathing. I pressed on and on, going faster all the time — not that I felt braver, but I longed to end the suspense. Suddenly the silence was broken by a threatening roar. It swept down on me, swelling as it continued, and it seemed to fill the cañon. It shook my pulses, it urged me to flight, but I could not move. Then as suddenly it ceased.

For a long moment I stood still, with no idea of advancing farther. The clinking of a chain seemed to release my cramped muscles. Very cautiously I peered around a projecting corner of wall. There sat a huge black bear on his haunches holding up a great steel trap which clutched one of his paws. It was such a strange sight that my fear was forgotten. There was something almost human in the way the bear looked at that trap. He touched it gingerly with his free paw, and nosed it. I crept up close to the corner of stone and looked around again. The bear was now close to me. I saw the heavy chain and the log to which it was attached. He looked at trap and log in a grave, pathetic way, as if trying to reason about them. Then he roused into furious action, swinging the trap, dragging the log, and bellowing in such a frightful manner that I dodged back behind the wall.

But this sudden change in the bear, this appalling roar with its note of pain, awakened me to his suffering. When the noise stopped and I looked again, the bear was a sight not to be forgotten. He showed a helpless, terrible fear of the steel-jawed thing on his foot. He dropped down on the sand with a groan, and there was a despairing look in his eyes.

This made me forget my fear, and I had only one thought — to put him out of his misery. When I levelled my rifle it was as steady as the rock beside me. Aiming just below his ear, I pressed the trigger. The dull report re-echoed from wall to wall. The bear lurched slightly, and his head fell upon his outstretched paws. I waited, ready to shoot again upon the slightest movement, but there was none.

With rifle ready I cautiously approached the bear. As I came close he seemed larger and larger, but he showed no signs of life. I looked at the glossy black fur, the flecks of blood on the side of his head where my bullet had entered, the murderous saw-teeth of the heavy trap biting to the bone, and the cruelty of that trap seemed to drive from me all pride of achievement. It was nothing except mercy to kill a trapped crippled bear that could not run or fight. Then and there I gained a dislike for trapping animals.

The crack of the old hunter's rifle made me remember that I was to hurry back up the other cañon, so I began to run. I bounded from stone to stone, dashed over the sand-bars, jumped the brook, and went down that cañon perhaps in far greater danger of bodily harm than when I had gone up.

But when I turned the corner it was another story. The first cañon had been easy climbing compared to this one. It was narrow, steep, and full of dead pines fallen from above. Running was impossible. I clambered upward over the loose stones, under the bridges of pines, round the bowlders. Presently I heard a shout. I could not tell where it came from, but I replied. A second call I identified as coming from high up the ragged cañon side, and I started up. It was hard work. Certainly no bears or hunter had climbed out just there. At length, sore, spent, and torn, I fell out of a tangle of brush upon the edge of the cañon. Above me rose the swelling mountain slope thickly covered with dwarf pines.

"This way, youngster!" called the old hunter from my left.

A few more dashes in and out of the brush and trees brought me to a fairly open space with not much slope. Hiram Bent stood under a pine, and at his feet lay a black furry mass.

"Wal, I heerd you shoot. Reckon you got yourn?"

"Yes, I killed him. . . . Say, Mr. Bent, I don't like traps."

"Nary do I — for bears," replied he, shaking his gray head. "A trapped bear is about the pitifulest thing I ever seen. But it's seldom one ever gits into trap of mine."

"This one you shot must be the old mother bear. Where's the cub? Did it get away?"

"Not yet. Look up in the tree."

I looked up the black trunk through the network of slender branches, and saw the bear snuggling in a fork. His sharp ears stood up against the sky. He was most anxiously gazing down at us.

"Wal, tumble him out of thar," said Hiram Bent.

With a natural impulse to shoot I raised my rifle, but the cub looked so attractive and so helpless that I hesitated.

"I don't like to do it," I said. "Oh, I wish we could catch him alive!"

"Wal, I reckon we can."

"How?" I inquired, eagerly, and lowered my rifle.

"Are you good on the climb?"

"Climb? This tree? Why, with one hand. Back in Pennsylvania I climbed shell-bark hickory-trees with the lowest limb fifty feet from the ground. . . But there weren't any bears up them."

"You must keep out of his way if he comes down on you. He's a sassy little chap. Now take this rope an' go up an' climb round him."

"Climb round him?" I queried, as I gazed dubiously upward. "You mean to slip out on the branches and go up hand-over-hand till I get above him. The branches up there seem pretty close — I might. But suppose he goes higher?"

"I'm lookin' fer him to go clean to the top. But you can beat him to it — mebbe."

"Any danger of his attacking me — up there?"

"Wal, not much. If he hugs the trunk he'll have to hold on fer all he's worth. But if he stands on the branches an' you come up close he might bat you one. Mebbe I'd better go up."

"Oh, I'm going — I only wanted to know what to expect. Now, in case I get above him, what then?"

"Make him back down till he reaches these first branches. When he gets so far I'll tell you what to do."

I put my arm through the coil of rope, and, slinging it snugly over my shoulder, began to climb the pine. It was the work of only a moment to reach the first branch.

"Wal, I reckon you're some relation to a squirrel at thet," said Hiram Bent. "Jest as I thought — the little cuss is climbin' higher. Thet's goin' to worry us."

It was like stepping up a ladder from the first branch to the fork. The cub had gone up the right-hand trunk some fifteen feet, and was now hugging it. At that short distance he looked alarmingly big. But I saw he would have all he could do to hold on, and if I could climb the left trunk and get above him there would be little to fear. How I did it so quickly was a mystery, but amid the cracking of dead branches and pattering of falling bark and swaying of the tree-top I gained a position above him.

He was so close that I could smell him. His quick little eyes snapped fire and fear at once; he uttered a sound that was between a whine and a growl.

"Hey, youngster!" yelled Hiram, "thet's high enough — 'tain't safe — be careful now."

With the words I looked out below me, to see the old hunter standing in the glade waving his arms.

"I'm all right!" I yelled down. "Now, how'll I drive him?"

"Break off a branch an' switch him."

There was not a branch above me that I could break, but a few feet below was a slender, dead limb. I slid down and got it, and, holding on with my left arm and legs, I began to thrash the cub. He growled fiercely, snapped at the stick, and began to back down.

"He's started!" I cried, in glee. "Go on, Cubby — down with you!"

Clumsy as he was, he made swift time. I was hard put to keep close to him. I slipped down the trunk, holding on one instant and sliding down the next. But below the fork it was harder for Cubby and easier for me. The branches rather hindered his backward progress while they aided me. Growling and whining, with long claws ripping the bark, he went down. All of a sudden I became aware of the old hunter threshing about under the tree.

"Hold on — not so fast!" he yelled.

Still the cub kept going, and stopped with his haunches on the first branch. There, looking down, he saw an enemy below him, and hesitated. But he looked up, and, seeing me, began to back down again. Hiram pounded the tree with a dead branch. Cubby evidently intended to reach the ground, for the noise did not stop him. Then the hunter ran a little way to a windfall, and came back with the upper half of a dead sapling. With this he began to prod the bear. Thereupon, Cubby lost no time in getting up to the first branch again, where he halted.

"Throw the noose on him now — anywhere," ordered the hunter. "An' we've no time to lose. He's gittin' sassier every minnit."

I dropped the wide loop upon Cubby, expecting to catch him first time. The rope went over his head, but with a dexterous flip of his paw he sent it flying. Then began a duel between us, in which he continually got the better of me. All the while the old hunter prodded Cubby from below.

"You ain't quick enough," said Hiram, impatiently.

Made reckless by this, I stepped down to another branch directly over the bear, and tried again to rope him. It was of no use. He slipped out of the noose with the sinuous movements of an eel. Once it caught over his ears and in his open jaws. He gave a jerk that nearly pulled me from my perch. I could tell he was growing angrier every instant, and also braver. Suddenly the noose, quite by accident, caught his nose. He wagged his head and I pulled. The noose tightened.

"I've got him!" I yelled, and gave the rope a strong pull.

The bear stood up with startling suddenness and reached for me.

"Climb!" shouted Hiram.

I dropped the rope and leaped for the branch above, and, catching it, lifted myself just as the sharp claws of the cub scratched hard over my boot.

Cubby now hugged the tree trunk and started up again.

"We've got him!" yelled Hiram. "Don't move — step on his nose if he gets too close."

Then I saw the halter had come off the bear and had fallen to the ground. Hiram picked it up, arranged the noose, and, holding it in his teeth, began to climb after the bear. Cubby was now only a few feet under me, working steadily up, growling, and his little eyes were like points of green fire.

"Stop him! Stand on his head!" mumbled Hiram, with the rope in his teeth.

"What! — not on your life!"

But, reaching up, I grasped a branch, and, swinging clear of the lower one, I began to kick at the bear. This stopped him. Then he squealed, and began to kick on his own account. Hiram was trying to get the noose over a hind foot. After several attempts he succeeded, and then threw the rope over the lowest branch. I gave a wild Indian yell of triumph. The next instant, before I could find a foothold, the branch to which I was hanging snapped like a pistol-shot, and I plunged down with a crash. I struck the bear and the lower branch, and then the ground. The fall half stunned me. I thought every bone in my body was broken. I rose unsteadily, and for a moment everything whirled before my eyes. Then I discovered that the roar in my ears was the old hunter's yell. I saw him hauling on the rope. There was a great ripping of bark and many strange sounds, and then the cub was dangling head downward. Hiram had pulled him from his perch, and hung him over the lowest branch.

"Thar, youngster, git busy now!" yelled the hunter. "Grab the other rope — thar it is — an' rope a front paw while I hold him. Lively now, he's mighty heavy, an' if he ever gits down with only one rope on him we'll think we're fast to chain lightnin'."

The bear swung about five feet from the ground. As I ran at him with the noose he twisted himself, seemed to double up in a knot, then he dropped full-stretched again, and lunged viciously at me. Twice I felt the wind of his paws. He spun around so fast that it kept me dancing. I flung the noose and caught his right paw. Hiram bawled something that made me all the more heedless, and in tightening the noose I ran in too close. The bear gave me a slashing cuff on the side of the head, and I went down like a tenpin.

"Git a hitch thar — to the saplin'!" roared Hiram, as I staggered to my feet. "Rustle now — hurry!"

What with my ringing head, and fingers all thumbs, and Hiram roaring at me, I made a mess of tying the knot. Then Hiram let go his rope, and when the cub dropped to the ground the rope flew up over the branch. Cubby leaped so quickly that he jerked the rope away before Hiram could pick it up, and one hard pull loosened my hitch on the sapling.

The cub bounded through the glade, dragging me with him. For a few long leaps I kept my feet, then down I sprawled.

"Hang on! Hang on!" Hiram yelled from behind.

If I had not been angry clear through at that cub I might have let go. He ploughed my face in the dirt, and almost jerked my arms off. Suddenly the strain lessened. I got up, to see that the old hunter had hold of the other rope.

"Now, stretch him out!" he yelled.

Between us we stretched the cub out, so that all he could do was struggle and paw the air and utter strange cries. Hiram tied his rope to a tree, and then ran back to relieve me. It was high time. He took my rope and fastened it to a stout bush.

"Thar, youngster, I reckon thet'll hold him! Now tie his paws an' muzzle him."

He drew some buckskin thongs from his pocket and handed them to me. We went up to the straining cub, and Hiram, with one pull of his powerful hands, brought the hind legs together.

"Tie 'em," he said.

This done, with the aid of a heavy piece of wood he pressed the cub's head down and wound a thong tightly round the sharp nose. Then he tied the front legs.

"Thar! Now you loosen the ropes an' wind them up."

When I had done this he lifted the cub and swung him over his broad back.

"Come on, you trail behind, an' keep your eye peeled to see he doesn't work thet knot off his jaws. . . . Say, youngster, now you've got him, what in thunder will you do with him?"

I looked at my torn trousers, at the blood on my skinned and burning hands, and I felt of the bruise on my head, as I said, grimly:

"I'll hang to him as long as I can."

XIII

The Cabin in the Forest

Hiram Bent packed the cub down the cañon as he would have handled a sack of oats. When we reached the cabin he fastened a heavy dog-collar round Cubby's neck and snapped a chain to it. Doubling the halter, he tied one end to the chain and the other to a sturdy branch of a tree. This done, he slipped the thongs off the bear.

"Thar! He'll let you pet him in a few days — mebbe," he said.

Our captive did not yet show any signs of becoming tame. No sooner was he free of the buckskin thongs than he leaped away, only to be pulled up by the halter. Then he rolled over and over, clawing at the chain, and squirming to get his head out of the collar.

"He might choke hisself," said Hiram, "but mebbe he'll ease up if we stay away from him. Now we've got to rustle to skin them two bears."

So, after giving me a hunting-knife, and telling me to fetch my rifle, he set off up the cañon. As I trudged along behind him I spoke of Dick Leslie, and asked if there were not some way to get him out of the clutches of the lumber thieves.

"I've been thinkin' about thet," replied the hunter, "an' I reckon we can. To-morrow we'll cross the ridge high up back of thet spring-hole cañon, an' sneak down. 'Pears to me them fellers will be trailin' you pretty hard, an' mebbe they'll leave only one to guard Leslie. More'n thet, the trail up here to my shack is known, an' I'm thinkin' we'd be smart to go off an' camp somewhere else."

"What'll I do about Cubby?" I asked, quickly.

"Cubby? Oh, thet bear cub. Wal, take him along. Youngster, you don't want to pack thet pesky cub back to Pennsylvania?"

"Yes, I do."

"I reckon it ain't likely you can. He's pretty heavy. Weighs nearly a hundred. An' he'd make a heap of trouble. Mebbe we'll ketch a little cub — one you can carry in your arms."

"That'd be still better," I replied. "But if we don't, I'll try to take him back home."

The old hunter said I made a good shot at the big bear, and that he would give me the skin for a rug. It delighted me to think of that huge glossy bearskin on the floor of my den. I told Hiram how the bear had suffered, and I was glad to see that, although he was a hunter and trapper, he disliked to catch a bear in a trap. We skinned the animal, and cut out a quantity of meat. He told me that bear meat would make me forget all about venison. By the time we had climbed up the other cañon and skinned the other bear and returned to camp it was dark. As for me, I was so tired I could hardly crawl.

In spite of my aches and pains, that was a

night for me to remember. But there was the thought of Dick Leslie. His rescue was the only thing needed to make me happy. Dick was in my mind even when Hiram cooked a supper that almost made me forget my manners. Certainly the broiled bear meat made me forget venison. Then we talked before the burning logs in the stone fireplace. Hiram sat on his home-made chair and smoked a strong-smelling pipe while I lay on a bearskin in blissful ease. Occasionally we heard the cub outside rattling his chain and growling. All of the trappers and Indian fighters I had read of were different from Hiram Bent and Jim Williams. Jim's soft drawl and kind, twinkling eyes were not what any book-reader would expect to find in a dangerous man. And Hiram Bent was so simple and friendly, so glad to have even a boy to talk to, that it seemed he would never stop. If it had not been for his striking appearance and for the strange, wild tales he told of his lonely life, he would have reminded me of the old canal-lock tenders at home.

Once, when he was refilling his pipe and I thought it would be a good time to profit from his knowledge of the forests, I said to him:

"Now, Mr. Bent, let's suppose I'm the President of the United States, and I have just appointed you to the office of Chief Forester of the National Forests. You have full power. The object is to conserve our national resources. What will you do?"

"Wal, Mr. President," he began, slowly and

seriously, and with great dignity, "the Government must own the forests an' deal wisely with them. These mountain forests are great sponges to hold the water, an' we must stop fire an' reckless cuttin'. The first thing is to overcome the opposition of the stockmen, an' show them where the benefit will be theirs in the long run. Next the timber must be used, but not all used up. We'll need rangers who're used to rustlin' in the West an' know Western ways. Cabins must be built, trails made, roads cut. We'll need a head forester for every forest. This man must know all that's on his preserve, an' have it mapped. He must teach his rangers what he knows about trees. Penetier will be given over entirely to the growin' of yellow pine. Thet thrives best, an' the parasites must go. All dead an' old timber must be cut, an' much of thet where the trees are crowded. The north slopes must be cut enough to let in the sun an' light. Brush, windfalls, rottin' logs must be burned. Thickets of young pine must be thinned. Care oughter be taken not to cut on the north an' west edges of the forests, as the old guard pines will break the wind."

"How will you treat miners and prospectors?"

"They must be as free to take up claims as if there wasn't no National Forest."

"How about the settler, the man seeking a home out West?" I went on.

"We'll encourage him. The more men there are, the better the forester can fight fire. But these home-seekers must want a home, an' not be squattin' for a little, jest to sell out to lumber sharks."

"What's to become of timber and wood?"

"Wal, it's there to be used, an' must be used. We'll give it free to the settler an' prospector. We'll sell it cheap to the lumbermen — big an' little. We'll consider the wants of the local men first."

"Now about the range. Will you keep out the stockmen?"

"Nary. Grazin' for sheep, cattle, an' hosses will go on jest the same. But we must look out for overgrazin'. For instance, too many cattle will stamp down young growth, an' too many sheep leave no grazin' for other stock. The head forester must know his business, an' not let his range be overstocked. The small local herders an' sheepmen must be considered first, the big stockmen second. Both must be charged a small fee per head for grazin'."

"How will you fight fire?"

"Wal, thet's the hard nut to crack. Fire is the forest's worst enemy. In a dry season like this Penetier would burn like tinder blown by a bellows. Fire would race through here faster 'n a man could run. I'll need special fire rangers, an' all other rangers must be trained to fight fire, an' then any men living in or near the forest will be paid to help. The thing to do is watch for the small fires an' put them out. Campers must be made to put out their fires before leaving

135

camp. Brush piles an' slashes mustn't be burned in dry or windy weather."

Just where we left off talking I could not remember, for I dropped off to sleep. I seemed hardly to have closed my eyes when the hunter called me in the morning. The breakfast was smoking on the red-hot coals, and outside the cabin all was dense gray fog.

When, soon after, we started down the cañon, the fog was lifting and the forest growing lighter. Everything was as white with frost as if it had snowed. A thin, brittle frost crackled under our feet. When we had gotten below the rocky confines of the cañon we climbed the slope to the level ridge. Here it was impossible not to believe it had snowed. The forest was as still as night, and looked very strange with the white aisles lined by black tree trunks and the gray fog shrouding the tree-tops. Soon we were climbing again, and I saw that Hiram meant to head the cañon where I had left Dick.

The fog split and blew away, and the brilliant sunlight changed the forest. The frost began to melt, and the air was full of mist. We climbed and climbed — out of the stately yellow-pine zone, up among the gnarled and blasted spruces, over and around strips of weathered stone. Once I saw a cold, white snow-peak. It was hard enough for me to carry my rifle and keep up with the hunter without talking. Besides, Hiram had answered me rather shortly, and I thought it best to keep silent. From time to time he stopped to listen. Then when he turned to go down the slope he trod carefully, and cautioned me not to loosen stones, and he went slower and yet slower. From this I made sure we were not far from the spring-hole.

"Thar's the cañon," he whispered, stopping to point below, where a black, irregular line marked the gorge. "I haven't heerd a thing, an' we're close. Mebbe they're asleep. Mebbe most of them are trailin' you, an' I hope so. Now, don't you put your hand or foot on anythin' thet'll make a noise."

Then he slipped off, and it was wonderful to see how noiselessly he stepped, and how he moved between trees and dead branches without a sound. I managed pretty well, yet more than once a rattling stone or a broken branch stopped Hiram short and made him lift a warning hand.

At last we got down to the narrow bench which separated the cañon-slope from the deep cut. It was level and roughly strewn with bowlders. Here we took to all fours and crawled. It was easy to move here without noise, for the ground was rocky and hard, and there was no brush.

Suddenly I fairly bumped into the hunter. Looking up, I saw that he had halted only a few feet from the edge of the gorge where I had climbed out in my escape. He was listening. There was not a sound save the dull roar of rushing water.

Hiram slid forward a little, and rose cautiously

to look over. I did the same. When I saw the cave and the spring-hole I felt a catch in my throat.

But there was not a man in sight. Dick's captors had broken camp; they were gone. The only thing left in the gorge to show they had ever been there was a burned-out camp-fire.

"They're gone," I whispered.

"Wal, it 'pears so," replied Hiram. "An' it's a move I don't like. Youngster, it's you they want. Leslie's no particular use to them. They'll have to let him go sooner or later, if they hain't already."

"What'll we do now?"

"Make tracks. We'll cut back across the ridge an' git some blankets an' grub, then light out for the other side of Penetier."

I thought the old hunter had made rapid time on our way up, but now I saw what he really meant by "making tracks." Fortunately, after a short, killing climb, the return was all down-hill. One stride of Hiram's equalled two of mine, and he made his faster, so that I had to trot now and then to catch up. Very soon I was as hot as fire, and every step was an effort. But I kept thinking of Dick, of my mustang and outfit, and I vowed I would stick to Hiram Bent's trail till I dropped. For the matter of that, I did drop more than once before we reached the cabin.

A short rest while Hiram was packing a few things put me right again. I strapped my rifle over my shoulder, and then went out to untie my bear cub. It would have cost me a great deal to leave him behind. I knew I ought to, still I could not bring myself to it. All my life I had wanted a bear cub. Here was one that I had helped to lasso and tie up with my own hands. I made up my mind to hold to the cub until the last gasp.

So I walked up to Cubby with a manner more bold than sincere. He had not eaten anything, but he had drunk the water we had left for him. To my surprise he made no fuss when I untied the rope; on the other hand, he seemed to look pleased, and I thought I detected a cunning gleam in his little eyes. He paddled away down the cañon, and, as this was in the direction we wanted to go, I gave him slack rope and followed.

"Wal, you're goin' to have a right pert time, youngster, an' don't you forget it," said Hiram Bent.

The truth of that was very soon in evidence. Cubby would not let well enough alone, and he would not have a slack rope. I think he wanted to choke himself or pull my arms out. When I realized that Cubby was three times as strong as I was I began to see that my work was cut out for me. The more, however, that he jerked me and hauled me along, the more I determined to hang on. I thought I had a genuine love for him up to the time he had almost knocked my head off, but it was funny how easily he roused my anger after that. What would have happened had he taken a notion to go through the brush? Luckily he kept to the trail, which certainly was rough enough. So, with watching the cub and keeping my feet free of roots and rocks, I had no chance to look ahead. Still I had no concern about this, for the old hunter was at my heels, and I knew he would keep a sharp lookout.

Before I was aware of it we had gotten out of the narrow cañon into a valley with well-timbered bottom, and open, slow-rising slopes. We were getting down into Penetier. Cubby swerved from the trail and started up the left slope. I did not want to go, but I had to keep with him, and that was the only way. The hunter strode behind without speaking, and so I gathered that the direction suited him. By leaning back on the rope I walked up the slope as easily as if it were a moving stairway. Cubby pulled me up; I had only to move my feet. When we reached a level once more I discovered that the cub was growing stronger and wanted to go faster. We zigzagged across the ridge to the next cañon, which at a glance I saw was deep and steep.

"Thet'll be some work goin' down thar!" called Hiram. "Let me pack your gun."

I would have been glad to give it to him, but how was I to manage? I could not let go of the rope, and Hiram, laden as he was, could not catch up with me. Then suddenly it was too late, for Cubby lunged forward and down.

This first downward jump was not vicious — only a playful one perhaps, by way of initiating me; but it upset me, and I was dragged in the pine-needles. I did not leap to my feet; I was jerked up. Then began a wild chase down that steep, bushy slope. Cubby got going, and I could no more have checked him than I could a steam-engine. Very soon I saw that not only was the bear cub running away, but he was running away with me. I slid down yellow places where the earth was exposed, I tore through thickets, I dodged a thousand trees. In some grassy descents it was as if I had seven-league boots. I must have broken all records for jumps. All at once I stumbled just as Cubby made a spurt and flew forward, alighting face downward. I dug up the pine-needles with my outstretched hands, I scraped with my face and ploughed with my nose, I ate the dust; and when I brought up with a jolt against a log a more furious boy than Ken Ward it would be hard to imagine. Leaping up, I strove with every ounce of might to hold in the bear. But though fury lent me new strength, he kept the advantage.

Presently I saw the bottom of the cañon, an open glade, and an old log-cabin. I looked back to see if the hunter was coming. He was not in sight, but I fancied I heard him. Then Cubby, putting on extra steam, took the remaining rods of the slope in another spurt. I had to race, then fly, and at last lost my footing and plunged down into a thicket.

There farther progress stopped for both of us. Cubby had gone down on one side of a sapling and I on the other, with the result that we were brought up short. I crashed through some low bushes and bumped squarely into the cub. Whether it was his frantic effort to escape, or just excitement, or deliberate intention to beat me into a jelly I had no means to tell. The fact was he began to dig at me and paw me and maul me. Never had I been so angry. I began to fight back, to punch and kick him.

Suddenly, with a crashing in the bushes, the cub was hauled away from me, and then I saw Hiram at the rope.

"Wal, wal!" he ejaculated, "your own mother wouldn't own you now!"

Then he laughed heartily and chuckled to himself, and gave the cub a couple of jerks that took the mischief out of him. I dragged myself after Hiram into the glade. The cabin was large and very old, and part of the roof was sunken in.

"We'll hang up here an' camp," said Hiram. "This is an old hunters' cabin, an' kinder out of the way. We'll hitch this little fighter inside, where mebbe he won't be so noisy."

The hunter hauled the cub up short, and half pulled, half lifted him into the door. I took off my rifle, emptied my pockets of brush and beat out the dust, and combed the pine-needles from my hair. My hands were puffed and red, and smarted severely. And altogether I was in no amiable frame of mind as regarded my captive bear cub.

When I stepped inside the cabin it was dark,

and coming from the bright light I could not for a moment see what the interior looked like. Presently I made out one large room with no opening except the door. There was a tumble-down stone fireplace at one end, and at the other a rude ladder led up to a loft. Hiram had thrown his pack aside, and had tied Cubby to a peg in the log wall.

"Wal, I'll fetch in some fresh venison," said the hunter. "You rest awhile, an' then gather some wood an' make a fire."

The rest I certainly needed, for I was so tired I could scarcely untie the pack to get out the blankets. The bear cub showed signs of weariness, which pleased me. It was not long after Hiram's departure that I sank into a doze.

When my eyes opened I knew I had been awakened by something, but I could not tell what. I listened. Cubby was as quiet as a mouse, and his very quiet and the alert way he held his ears gave me a vague alarm. He had heard something. I thought of the old hunter's return, yet this did not reassure me.

All at once the voices of men made me sit up with a violent start. Who could they be? Had Hiram met a ranger? I began to shake a little, and was about to creep to the door when I heard the clink of stirrups and soft thud of hoofs. Then followed more voices, and last a loud volley of curses.

"Herky-Jerky!" I gasped, and looked about wildly.

I had no time to dash out of the door. I was caught in a trap, and I felt cold and sick. Suddenly I caught sight of the ladder leading to the loft. Like a monkey I ran up, and crawled as noiselessly as possible upon the rickety flooring of dry pine branches. Then I lay there quivering.

XIV

A Prisoner

It chanced that as I lay on my side my eye caught a gleam of light through a little ragged hole in the matting of pine branches. Part of the interior of the cabin, the doorway, and some space outside were plainly visible. The thud of horses had given place to snorts, and then came a flopping of saddles and packs on the ground.

"Any water hyar?" asked a gruff voice I recognized as Bill's.

"Spring right thar," replied a voice I knew to be Bud's.

"You onery old cayuse, stand still!"

From that I gathered Herky was taking the saddle off his horse.

"Here, Leslie, I'll untie you — if you'll promise not to bolt."

That voice was Buell's. I would have known it among a thousand. And Dick was still a prisoner.

"Bolt! If you let me loose I'll beat your fat head off!" replied Dick. "Ha! A lot you care about my sore wrists. You're weakening, Buell, and you know it. You've got a yellow streak."

"Shet up!" said Herky, in a low, sharp tone. A silence followed. "Buell, look hyar in the trail.

Tracks! Goin' in an' comin' out."

"How old are they?"

"I'll bet a hoss they ain't an hour old."

"Somebody's usin' the cabin, eh?"

The men then fell to whispering, and I could not understand what was said, but I fancied they were thinking only of me. My mind worked fast. Buell and his fellows had surely not run across Hiram Bent. Had the old hunter deserted me? I flouted such a thought. It was next to a certainty that he had seen the lumbermen, and for reasons best known to himself had not returned to the cabin. But he was out there somewhere among the pines, and I did not think any of those ruffians was safe.

Then I heard stealthy footsteps approaching. Soon I saw the Mexican slipping cautiously to the door. He peeped within. Probably the interior was dark to him, as it had been to me. He was not a coward, for he stepped inside.

At that instant there was a clinking sound, a rush and a roar, and a black mass appeared to hurl itself upon the Mexican. He went down with a piercing shriek. Then began a fearful commotion. Screams and roars mingled with the noise of combat. I saw a whirling cloud of dust on the cabin floor. The cub had jumped on the Mexican. What an unmerciful beating he was giving that Greaser! I could have yelled out in my glee. I had to bite my tongue to keep from urging on my docile little pet bear. Greaser surely thought he had fallen in with his evil spirit, for he howled to the saints to save him.

Herky-Jerky was the only one of his companions brave enough to start to help him.

"The cabin's full of b'ars!" he yelled.

At his cry the bear leaped out of the cloud of dust, and shot across the threshold like black lightning. In his onslaught upon Greaser he had broken his halter. Herky-Jerky stood directly in his path. I caught only a glimpse, but it served to show that Herky was badly scared. The cub dove at Herky, under him, straight between his legs like a greased pig, and, spilling him all over the trail, sped on out of sight. Herky raised himself, and then he sat there, red as a lobster, and bawled curses while he made his huge revolver spurt flame on flame.

I could not see the other men, but their uproarious mirth could have been heard half a mile away. When it dawned upon Herky, he was so furious that he spat at them like an angry cat and clicked his empty revolver.

Then Greaser lurched out of the door. I got a glimpse of him, and, for a wonder, was actually sorry for him. He looked as if he had been through a threshing-machine.

"Haw! haw! Ho! ho!" roared the merry lumbermen.

Then they trooped into the cabin. Buell headed the line, and Herky, sullenly reloading his revolver, came last. At first they groped around in the dim light, stumbling over everything. Part of the time they were in the light space near the door, and the rest I could not see them. I scarcely dared to breathe. I felt a creepy chill, and my eyesight grew dim.

"Who does this stuff belong to, anyhow?" Buell was saying. "An' what was thet bear doin' in here?"

"He was roped up — hyar's the hitch," answered Bud.

"An' hyar's a rifle — Winchester — ain't been used much. Buell, it's thet kid's!"

I heard rapid footsteps and smothered exclamations.

"Take it from me, you're right!" ejaculated Buell. "We jest missed him. Herky, them tracks out there? Somebody's with this boy — who?"

"It's Jim Williams," put in Dick Leslie, cool-voiced and threatening.

The little stillness that followed his words was broken by Buell.

"Naw! 'Twasn't Williams. You can't bluff this bunch, Leslie. By your own words Williams is lookin' for us, an' if he's lookin' for anybody I know he's lookin' for 'em. See!"

"Buell, the kid's fell in with old Bent, the b'ar-hunter," said Bill. "Thet accounts fer the cub. Bent's allus got cubs, an' kittens, an' sich. An' I'll tell you, he ain't no better friend of ourn than Jim Williams."

"I'd about as soon tackle Williams as Bent," put in Bud.

Buell shook his fist. "What luck the kid has!

But I'll get him, take it from me! Now, what's best to do?"

"Buell, the game's going against you," said Dick Leslie. "The penitentiary is where you'll finish. You'd better let me loose. Old Bent will find Jim Williams, and then you fellows will be up against it. There's going to be somebody killed. The best thing for you to do is to let me go and then cut out yourself."

Buell breathed as heavily as a porpoise, and his footsteps pounded hard.

"Leslie, I'm seein' this out — understand? When Bud rode down to the mill an' told me the kid had got away I made up my mind to ketch him an' shet his mouth — one way or another. An' I'll do it. Take thet from me!"

"Bah!" sneered Dick. "You're scared into the middle of next week right now. . . . Besides, if you do ketch Ken it won't do you any good — now!"

"*What?*"

But Dick shut up like a clam, and not another word could be gotten from him. Buell fumed and stamped.

"Bud, you're the only one in this bunch of logger-heads thet has any sense. What d'you say?"

"Quiet down an' wait here," replied Bud. "Mebbe old Bent didn't hear them shots of Herky's. He may come back. Let's wait awhile, an', if he doesn't come, put Herky on the trail."

"Good! Greaser, go out an' hide the hosses

— drive them up the cañon."

The Mexican shuffled out, and all the others settled down to quiet. I heard some of them light their pipes. Bud leaned against the left of the door, Buell sat on the other side, and beyond them I saw as much of Herky as his boots. I knew him by his bow-legs.

The stillness that set in began to be hard on me. When the men were moving about and talking I had been so interested that my predicament did not occupy my mind. But now, with those ruffians waiting silently below, I was beset with a thousand fears. The very consciousness that I must be quiet made it almost impossible. Then I became aware that my one position cramped my arm and side. A million prickling needles were at my elbow. A band as of steel tightened about my breast. I grew hot and cold, and trembled. I knew the slightest move would be fatal, so I bent all my mind to lying quiet as a stone.

Greaser came limping back into the cabin, and found a seat without any one speaking. It was so still that I heard the silken rustle of paper as he rolled a cigarette. Moments that seemed long as years passed, with my muscles clamped as in a vise. If only I had lain down upon my back! But there I was, half raised on my elbow, in a most awkward and uncomfortable position. I tried not to mind the tingling in my arm, but to think of Hiram, of Jim, of my mustang. But presently I could not think of anything except the certainty that I would soon lose control of my muscles and fall over.

The tingling changed to a painful vibration, and perspiration stung my face. The strain became unbearable. All of a sudden something seemed to break within me, and my muscles began to ripple and shake. I had no power to stop it. More than that, the feeling was so terrible that I knew I would welcome discovery as a relief.

"Sh-s-s-h!" whispered some one below.

I turned my eyes down to the peep-hole. Bud had moved over squarely into the light of the door. He was bending over something. Then he extended his hand, back uppermost, toward Buell. On the back of that broad brown hand were pieces of leaf and bits of pine-needles. The trembling of my body had shaken these from the brush on the rickety loft. More than that, in the yellow bar of sunlight which streamed in at the door there floated particles of dust.

Bud silently looked upward. There was a gleam in his black eyes, and his mouth was agape. Buell's gaze followed Bud's, and his face grew curious, intent, then fixed in a cunning, bold smile of satisfaction. He rose to his feet.

"Come down out o' thet!" he ordered, harshly. "Come down!"

The sound of his voice stilled my trembling. I did not move nor breathe. I saw Buell loom up hugely and Bud slowly rise. Herky-Jerky's boots suddenly stood on end, and I knew then he had also risen. The silence which followed

Buell's order was so dense that it oppressed me.

"Come down!" repeated Buell.

There was no hint of doubt in his deep voice, but a cold certainty and a brutal note. I had feared the man before, but that gave me new terror.

"Bud, climb the ladder," commanded Buell.

"I ain't stuck on thet job," rejoined Bud.

As his heavy boots thumped on the ladder they jarred the whole cabin. My very desperation filled me with the fierceness of a cornered animal. I caught sight of a short branch of the thickness of a man's arm, and, grasping it, I slowly raised myself. When Bud's black, round head appeared above the loft I hit it with all my might.

Bud bawled like a wounded animal, and fell to the ground with the noise of a load of bricks. Through my peep-hole I saw him writhing, with both hands pressed to his head. Then, lying flat on his back, he whipped out his revolver. I saw the red spurt, the puff of smoke. Bang!

A bullet zipped through the brush, and tore a hole through the roof.

Bang! Bang!

I felt a hot, tearing pain in my arm.

"Stop, you black idiot!" yelled Buell. He kicked the revolver out of Bud's hand. "What d'you mean by thet?"

In the momentary silence that followed I listened intently, even while I held tightly to my arm. From its feeling my arm seemed to be shot off, but it was only a flesh-wound. After the first instant of shock I was not scared. But blood flowed fast. Warm, oily, slippery, it ran down inside my shirt-sleeve and dripped off my fingers.

"Bud," hoarsely spoke up Bill, breaking the stillness, "mebbe you killed him!"

Buell coughed, as if choking.

"What's thet?" For once his deep voice was pitched low. "Listen."

Drip! drip! drip! It was like the sound of water dripping from a leak in a roof. It was directly under me, and, quick as thought, I knew the sound was made by my own dripping blood.

"Find thet, somebody," ordered Buell.

Drip! drip! drip!

One of the men stepped noisily.

"Hyar it is — thar," said Bill. "Look on my hand. . . . Blood! I knowed it. Bud got him, all right."

There was a sudden rustling such as might come from a quick, strained movement.

"Buell," cried Dick Leslie, in piercing tones, "Heaven help you murdering thieves if that boy's killed! I'll see you strung up right in this forest. Ken, speak! Speak!"

It seemed then, in my pain and bitterness, that I would rather let Buell think me dead. Dick's voice went straight to my heart, but I made no answer.

"Leslie, I didn't kill him, an' I didn't order it," said Buell, in a voice strangely shrunk and shaken. "I meant no harm to the lad. . . . Go up, Bud, an' get him."

Bud made no move, nor did Greaser when he was ordered.

"Go up, somebody, an' see what's up there!" shouted Buell.

"Strikes me you might go yourself," said Bill, coolly.

With a growl Buell mounted the ladder. When his great shock head hove in sight I was seized by a mad desire to give him a little of his own medicine. With both hands I lifted the piece of pine branch and brought it down with every ounce of strength in me.

Like a pistol it cracked on Buell's head and snapped into bits. The lumberman gave a smothered groan, then clattered down the ladder and rolled on the floor. There he lay quiet.

"All-fired dead — thet kid — now, ain't he?" said Bud, sarcastically. "How'd you like thet crack on the knob? You'll need a larger size hat, mebbe. Herky-Jerky, you go up an' see what's up there."

"I've a pictur of myself goin'," replied Herky, without moving.

"Whar's the water? Get some water, Greaser," chimed in Bill.

From the way they worked over Buell I concluded he had been pretty badly stunned. But he came to presently.

"What struck me?" he asked.

"Oh, nothin'," replied Bud, derisively. "The

loft up thar's full of air, an' it blowed on you, thet's all."

Buell got up, and began walking around.

"Bill, go out an' fetch in some long poles," he said.

When Bill returned with a number of sharp, bayonet-like pikes I knew the game was all up for me. Several of the men began to prod through the thin covering of dry brush. One of them reached me, and struck so hard that I lurched violently.

That was too much for the rickety loft floor. It was only a bit of brush laid on a netting of slender poles. It creaked, rasped, and went down with a crash. I alighted upon somebody, and knocked him to the floor. Whoever it was, seized me with iron hands. I was buried, almost smothered, in the dusty mass. My captor began to curse cheerfully, and I knew then that Herky-Jerky had made me a prisoner.

XV

The Fight

Herky hauled me out of the brush, and held me in the light. The others scrambled from under the remains of the loft, and all viewed me curiously.

"Kid, you ain't hurt much?" queried Buell, with concern.

I would have snapped out a reply, but I caught sight of Dick's pale face and anxious eyes.

"Ken," he called, with both gladness and doubt in his voice, "you look pretty good — but that blood. . . . Tell me, quick!"

"It's nothing, Dick, only a little cut. The bullet just ticked my arm."

Whatever Dick's reply was it got drowned in Herky-Jerky's long explosion of strange language. Herky was plainly glad I had not been badly hurt. I had already heard mirth, anger, disgust, and fear in his outbreaks, and now relief was added. He stripped off my coat, cut off the bloody sleeve of my shirt, and washed the wound. It was painful and bled freely, but it was not much worse than cuts from spikes when playing ball. Herky bound it tightly with a strip of my shirt-sleeve, and over that my handkerchief.

"Thar, kid, thet'll stiffen up an' be sore fer a day or two, but it ain't nothin'. You'll soon be bouncin' clubs offen our heads."

It was plain that Herky — and the others, for that matter, except Buell — thought more of me because I had wielded a club so vigorously.

"Look at thet lump, kid," said Bud, bending his head. "Now, ain't thet a nice way to treat a feller? It made me plumb mad, it did."

"I'm likely to hurt somebody yet," I declared.

They looked at me curiously. Buell raised his face with a queer smile. Bud broke into a laugh.

"Oh, you're *goin'* to? Mebbe you think you need an axe," said he.

They made no offer to tie me up then. Bud went to the door and sat in it, and I heard him half whisper to Buell: "What'd I tell you? Thet's a game kid. If he ever wakes up right we'll have a wildcat on our hands. He'll do fer one of us yet." These men all took pleasure in saying things like this to Buell. This time Buell had no answer ready, and sat nursing his head. "Wal, I hev a little headache myself, an' the crack I got wasn't nothin' to yourn," concluded Bud. Then Bill began packing the supplies indoors, and Herky started a fire. Bud kept a sharp eye on me; still, he made no objection when I walked over and lay down upon the blankets near Dick.

"Dick, I shot a bear and helped to tie up a cub," I said. And then I told him all that had happened from the time I scrambled out of the spring-hole till I was discovered up in the loft.

Dick shook his head, as if he did not know what to make of me, and all he said was that he would give a year's pay to have me safe back in Pennsylvania.

Herky-Jerky announced supper in his usual manner — a challenge to find as good a cook as he was, and a cheerful call to "grub." I did not know what to think of his kindness to me. Remembering how he had nearly drowned me in the spring, I resented his sudden change. He could not do enough for me. I asked the reason for my sudden popularity.

Herky scratched his head and grinned. "Yep, kid, you sure hev riz in my estimashun."

"Hey, you rummy cow-puncher!" broke in Bud, scornfully. "Mebbe you'd like the kid more'n you do if you'd got one of them wallops."

"Bud, I ain't sayin'," replied Herky, with his mouth full of meat. "Considerin' all points, howsoever, I'm thinkin' them wallops was distributed very proper."

They bandied such talk between them, and occasionally Bill chimed in with a joke. Greaser ate in morose silence. There must have been something on his mind. Buell took very little dinner, and appeared to be in pain. It was dark when the meal ended. Bud bound me up for the night, and he made a good job of it. My arm burned and throbbed, but not badly enough to prevent sleep. Twice I had nearly dropped off when loud laughs or voices roused me. My eyes closed with a picture of those rough, dark men sitting before the fire.

A noise like muffled thunder burst into my slumber. I awakened with my body cramped and stiff. It was daylight, and something had happened. Buell ran in and out of the cabin yelling at his men. All of them except Herky were wildly excited. Buell was abusing Bud for something, and Bud was blaming Buell.

"Thet's no way to talk to me!" said Bud, angrily. "He didn't break loose in my watch!"

"You an' Greaser had the job. Both of you went to sleep — take thet from me!"

"Wal, he's gone, an' he took the kid's gun with him," said Bill, coolly. "Now we'll be dodgin' bullets."

Dick Leslie had escaped! I could hardly keep down a cry of triumph. I did ask if it was true, but none of them paid any attention to me. Buell then ordered Herky-Jerky to trail Dick and see where he had gone. Herky refused point-blank.

"Nope. Not fer me," he said. "Leslie has a rifle. So has Bent, an' we haven't one among us. An', Buell, if Leslie falls in with Bent, it's goin' to git hot fer us round here."

This silenced Buell, but did not stop his restless pacings. His face was like a thunder-cloud, and he was plainly worried and harassed. Once Bud deliberately asked what he intended to do with me, and Buell snarled a reply which no one understood. His gloom extended to the others, except Herky, who whistled and sang as he busied himself about the camp-fire. Greaser appeared to be particularly cast down.

"Buell, what are you going to do with me?" I demanded. But he made no answer.

"Well, anyway," I went on, "somebody cut these ropes. I'm mighty sore and uncomfortable."

Herky-Jerky did not wait for permission; he untied me, and helped me to my feet. I was rather unsteady on my legs at first, and my injured arm felt like a board. It seemed dead; but after I had moved it a little the pain came back, and it had apparently come to stay. We ate breakfast, and then settled down to do nothing, or to wait for something to turn up. Buell sat in the doorway, moodily watching the trail. Once he spoke, ordering the Mexican to drive in the horses. I fancied from this that Buell might have decided to break camp, but there was no move to pack.

The morning quiet was suddenly split by the stinging crack of a rifle and a yell of agony.

Buell leaped to his feet, his ruddy face white.

"Greaser!" he exclaimed.

"Thet was about where Greaser cashed," replied Bill, coolly knocking the ashes from his pipe.

"No, Bill, you're wrong. Here comes Greaser, runnin' like an Indian."

"Look at the blood! He's been plugged, all right!" exclaimed Herky-Jerky.

The sound of running feet drew nearer, and

suddenly the group at the door broke to admit the Mexican. One side of his terrified face was covered with blood. His eyes were staring, his hands raised, he staggered as if about to fall.

"Señor Willi—am! Señor Willi—am!" he cried, and then called on Saint Somebody.

"Jim Williams! I said so," muttered Bud.

Bill caught hold of the excited Mexican, and pulled him nearer the light.

"Thet ain't a bad hurt. Jest cut his ear off!" said Bill. "Hyar, stand still, you wild man! You're not goin' to die. Git some water, Herky. Fellers, Greaser has been oneasy ever since he knew Jim Williams was lookin' fer him. He thinks Jim did this. But Jim Williams don't use a rifle, an', what's more, when he shoots he don't miss. You all heerd the rifle-shot."

"Then it was old Bent or Leslie?" questioned Buell.

"Leslie it were. Bent uses a 45-90 caliber. Thet shot we heerd was from the little 38 — the kid's gun."

"Wal, it was a narrer escape fer Greaser," said Bud. "Leslie's sore, an' he'll shoot fer keeps. Buell, you've started somethin'."

When Bill had washed the blood off the Mexican it was found that the ball had carried away the lower part of the ear, and with it, of course, the gold earring. The wound must have been extremely painful; it certainly took all the starch out of Greaser. He kept mumbling in his own language, and rolling his wicked black eyes and twisting his thin, yellow hands.

"What's to be done?" asked Buell, sharply.

"Thet's fer you to say," replied Bill, with his exasperating calmness.

"Must we hang up here to be shot at? Leslie's takin' a long chance on thet kid's life if he comes slingin' lead round this cabin."

Herky-Jerky spat tobacco-juice across the room and grunted. Then, with his beady little eyes as keen and cold as flint, he said: "Buell, Leslie knows you daren't harm the kid; an' as fer bullets, he'll take good care where he slings 'em. This deal of yours begins to look like a wild-goose stunt. It never was safe, an' now it's worse."

Here was even Herky-Jerky harping on Buell's situation. To me it did not appear much more serious than before. But evidently they thought so. Buell seemed on the verge of losing control of himself. He glared at Herky, and rammed his fists in his pockets and paced the long room. Presently he stepped out of the door.

A rifle cracked clear and sharp, another bellowed out heavy and hollow. A bullet struck the door-post, a second hummed through the door and thudded into the log wall. Buell jumped back into the room. His face worked, his breath hissed between his teeth, as with trembling hand he examined the front of his coat. A big bullet had torn through both lapels.

Bill stuck his pudgy finger in the hole. "The second bullet made thet. It was from old Hiram's gun — a 45-90."

"Bent an' Leslie! My God! They're shootin' to kill!" cried Buell.

"I should smile," replied Herky-Jerky.

Bud was peeping out through a chink between the logs. "I got their smoke," he said; "look, Bill, up the slope. They're too fur off, but we may as well send up respects." With that he aimed his revolver through the narrow crack and deliberately shot six times. The reports clapped like thunder, the smoke from burnt powder and the smell of brimstone filled the room. By way of reply old Hiram's rifle boomed out twice, and two heavy slugs crashed through the roof, sending down a shower of dust and bits of decayed wood.

"Thet's jist to show what a 45-90 can do," remarked Bill.

Bud reloaded his weapon while Bill shot several times. Herky-Jerky had his gun in hand, but contented himself with peering from different chinks between the logs. I hid behind the wide stone fire-place, and though I felt pretty safe from flying bullets, I began to feel the icy grip of fear. I had seen too much of these men in excitement, and knew if circumstances so brought it about there might come a moment when my life would not be worth a pin. They were all sober now, and deadly quiet. Buell showed the greatest alarm, though he had begun to settle down to what looked like fight. Herky was more fearless than any of them, and cooler even than Bill. All at once I missed the Mexican.

If he had not slipped out of the room he had hidden under the brush of the fallen loft or in a pile of blankets. But the room was smoky, and it was hard for me to be certain.

Some time passed with no shots and with no movement inside the cabin. Slowly the blue smoke wafted out of the door. The sunlight danced in gleams through the holes in the ragged roof. There was a pleasant swish of pine branches against the cabin.

"Listen," whispered Bud, hoarsely. "I heerd a pony snort."

Then the rapid beat of hard hoofs on the trail was followed by several shots from the hillside. Soon the clatter of hoofs died away in the distance.

"Who was thet?" asked three of Buell's men in unison.

"Take it from me, Greaser's sneaked," replied Buell.

"How'd he git out?"

With that Bud and Bill began kicking in the piles of brush.

"Aha! Hyar's the place," sang out Bud.

In one corner of the back wall a rotten log had crumbled, and here it was plain to all eyes that Greaser had slipped out. I remembered that on this side of the cabin there was quite a thick growth of young pine. Greaser had been able to conceal himself as he crawled toward the horses, and had probably been seen at the last moment. Herky-Jerky was the only one to make comment.

164

"I ain't wishin' Greaser any hard luck, but hope he carried away a couple of 45-90 slugs somewheres in his yeller carcass."

"It'd be worth a lot to the feller who can show me a way out of this mess," said Buell, mopping the beads of sweat from his face.

I got up — it seemed to me my mind was made up for me — and walked into the light of the room.

"Buell, I can show you the way," I said, quietly.

"What!" His mouth opened in astonishment. "Speak up, then."

The other men stepped forward, and I felt their eyes upon me.

"Let me go free. Let me out of here to find Dick Leslie. Then when you go to jail in Holston for stealing lumber I'll say a good word for you and your men. There won't be any charge of kidnapping or violence."

After a long pause, during which Buell bored me with gimlet eyes, he said, in a queer voice:

"Say thet again."

I repeated it, and added that he could not gain anything now by holding me a prisoner. I think he saw what I meant, but hated to believe it.

"It's too late," I said, as he hesitated.

"You mean Leslie lied an' you fooled me — you did get to Holston?" he shouted. He was quivering with rage, and the red flamed in his neck and face.

"Buell, I did get to Holston and I did send

165

word to Washington," I went on, hurriedly, for I had begun to lose my calmness. "I wrote to my father. He knows a friend of the Chief Forester who is close to the Department at Washington. By this time Holston is full of officers of the forest service. Perhaps they're already at your mill. Anyway, the game's up, and you'd better let me go."

Buell's face lost all its ruddy color, slowly blanched, and changed terribly. The boldness fled, leaving it craven, almost ghastly. Realizing he had more to fear from the law than conviction of his latest lumber steal, he made at me in blind anger.

"Hold on!" Herky-Jerky yelled, as he jumped between Buell and me.

Buell's breath was a hiss, and the words he bit between his clinched teeth were unintelligible. In that moment he would have killed me.

Herky-Jerky met his onslaught, and flung him back. Then, with his hand on the butt of his revolver, he spoke:

"Buell, hyar's where you an' me split. You've bungled your big deal. The kid stacked the deck on you. But I ain't a-goin' to see you do him harm fer it."

"Herky's right, boss," put in Bill, "thar's no sense in addin' murder to this mess. Strikes me you're in bad enough."

"So thet's your game? You're double-crossin' me now — all on a chance at kidnappin' for ransom money. Well, I'm through with the kid an' all of you. Take thet from me!"

"You skunk!" exclaimed Herky-Jerky, with the utmost cheerfulness.

"Wal, Buell," said Bill, in cool disdain, "cosiderin' my fondness fer fresh air an' open country, I can't say I'm sorry to dissolve future relashuns. I was only in jail once, an' I couldn't breathe free."

It was then Buell went beside himself with rage. He raised his huge fists, and shook himself, and plunged about the room, cursing. Suddenly he picked up an axe, and began chopping at the rotten log above the hole where Greaser had slipped out. Bud yelled at him, so did Bill; Herky-Jerky said unpleasant things. But Buell did not hear them. He hacked and dug away like one possessed. The dull, sodden blows fell fast, scattering pieces of wood about the floor. The madness that was in Buell was the madness to get out, to escape the consequences of his acts. His grunts and pants as he worked showed his desperate energy. Then he slammed the axe against the wall, and, going down flat, began to crawl through the opening. Buell was a thick man, and the hole appeared too small. He stuck in it, but he squeezed and flattened himself, finally worked through, and disappeared.

A sudden quiet fell upon his departure.

"Hands up!"

Jim Williams's voice! It was strange to see Herky and Bud flash up their arms without turning. But I wheeled quickly. Bill, too, had his hands high in the air.

In the sunlight of the doorway stood Jim Williams. Low down, carelessly, it seemed, he held two long revolvers. He looked the same easy, slow Texan I remembered. But the smile was not now in his eyes, and his lips were set in a thin, hard line.

XVI

The Forest's Greatest Foe

Jim Williams sent out a sharp call. From the cañon-slope came answering shouts. There were sounds of heavy bodies breaking through brush, followed by the thudding of feet. Then men could be plainly heard running up the trail. Jim leaned against the door-post, and the three fellows before him stood rigid as stone.

Suddenly a form leaped past Jim. It was Dick Leslie, bareheaded, his hair standing like a lion's mane, and he had a cocked rifle in his hands. Close behind him came old Hiram Bent, slower, more cautious, but no less formidable. As these, men glanced around with fiery eyes the quick look of relief that shot across their faces told of ungrounded fears.

"Where's Buell?" sharply queried Dick.

Jim Williams did not reply, and a momentary silence ensued.

"Buell lit out arter the Greaser," said Bill, finally.

"Cut and run, did he? That's his speed," grimly said Dick. "Here, Bent, find some rope. We've got to tie up these jacks."

"Hands back, an' be graceful like. Quick!" sang out Jim Williams.

It seemed to me human beings could not have more eagerly and swiftly obeyed an order. Herky and Bill and Bud jerked their arms down and extended their hands out behind. After that quick action they again turned into statues. There was a breathless suspense in every act. And there was something about Jim Williams then that I did not like. I was in a cold perspiration for fear one of the men would make some kind of move. As the very mention of the Texan had always caused a little silence, so his presence changed the atmosphere of that cabin room. Before his coming there had been the element of chance — a feeling of danger, to be sure, but a healthy spirit of give and take. That had all changed with Jim Williams's words "Hands up!" There was now something terrible hanging in the balance. I had but to look at Jim's eyes, narrow slits of blue fire, at the hard jaw and tight lips, to see a glimpse of the man who thought nothing of life. It turned me sick, and I was all in a tremor till Dick and Hiram had the men bound fast.

Then Jim dropped the long, blue guns into the holsters on his belt.

"Ken, I shore am glad to see yu," said he.

The soft, drawling voice, the sleepy smile, the careless good-will all came back, utterly transforming the man. This was the Jim Williams I had come to love. With a wrench I recovered myself.

"Are you all right, Ken?" asked Dick. And old

Hiram questioned me with a worried look. This anxiety marked the difference between these men and Williams. I hastened to assure my friends that I was none the worse for my captivity.

"Ken, your little gun doesn't shoot where it points," said Jim. "I shore had a bead on the Greaser an' missed him. First Greaser I ever missed."

"You shot his ear off," I replied. "He came running back covered with blood. I never saw a man so scared."

"Wal, I shore am glad," drawled Jim.

"He made off with your mustang," said Dick.

This information lessened my gladness at Greaser's escape. Still, I would rather have had him get away on my horse than stay to be shot by Jim.

Dick called me to go outside with him. My pack was lying under one of the pines near the cabin, and examination proved that nothing had been disturbed. We found the horses grazing up the cañon. Buell had taken the horse of one of his men, and had left his own superb bay. Most likely he had jumped astride the first animal he saw. Dick said I could have Buell's splendid horse. I had some trouble in catching him, as he was restive and spirited, but I succeeded eventually, and we drove the other horses and ponies into the glade. My comrades then fell to arguing about what to do with the prisoners. Dick was for packing them off to Holston. Bent talked against this, saying it was no easy matter to drive bound men over rough trails, and Jim sided with him.

Once, while they were talking, I happened to catch Herky-Jerky's eye. He was lying on his back in the light from the door. Herky winked at me, screwed up his face in the most astonishing manner, all of which I presently made out to mean that he wanted to speak to me. So I went over to him.

"Kid, you ain't a-goin' to fergit I stalled off Buell?" whispered Herky. "He'd hev done fer you, an' thet's no lie. You won't fergit when we're rustled down to Holston?"

"I'll remember, Herky," I promised, and I meant to put in a good word for him. Because, whether or not his reasons had to do with kidnapping and ransom, he had saved me from terrible violence, perhaps death.

It was decided that we would leave the prisoners in the cabin and ride down to the sawmill. Hiram was to return at once with officers. If none could be found at the mill he was to guard the prisoners and take care of them till Dick could send officers to relieve him. Thereupon we cooked a meal, and I was put to feeding Herky and his companions. Dick ordered me especially to make them drink water, as it might be a day or longer before Hiram could get back. I made Bill drink, and easily filled up Herky; but Bud, who never drank anything save whiskey, gave me a job. He refused with a growl, and I insisted with what I felt sure was Christian patience. Still he would not drink, so I put the cup to his lips and tipped it. Bud promptly spat the water all over me. And I as promptly got another cupful and dashed it all over him.

"Bud, you'll drink or I'll drown you," I declared.

So while Bill cracked hoarse jokes and Herky swore his pleasure, I made Bud drink all he could hold. Jim got a good deal of fun out of it, but Dick and Hiram never cracked a smile. Possibly the latter two saw something far from funny in the outlook; at any rate, they were silent, almost moody, and in a hurry to be off.

Dick was so anxious to be on the trail that he helped me pack my pony, and saddled Buell's horse. It was one thing to admire the big bay from the ground, and it was another to be astride him. Target — that was his name — had a spirited temper, an iron mouth, and he had been used to a sterner hand than mine. He danced all over the glade before he decided to behave himself. Riding him, however, was such a great pleasure that a more timid boy than I would have taken the risk. He would not let any horse stay near him; he pulled on the bridle, and leaped whenever a branch brushed him. I had been on some good horses, but never on one with a swing like his, and I grew more and more possessed with the desire to let him run.

"Like as not he'll bolt with you. Hold him in,

Ken!" called Dick, as he mounted. Then he shouted a final word to the prisoners, saying they would be looked after, and drove the pack-ponies into the trail. As we rode out we passed several of the horses that we had decided to leave behind, and as they wanted to follow us it was necessary to drive them back.

I had my hands full with the big, steel-jawed steed I was trying to hold in. It was the hardest work of the kind that I had ever undertaken. I had never worn spurs, but now I began to wish for them. We travelled at a good clip, as fast as the pack-ponies could go, and covered a long distance by camping-time. I was surprised that we did not get out of the cañon. The place where we camped was a bare, rocky opening, with a big pool in the centre. While we were making camp it suddenly came over me that I was completely bewildered as to our where-abouts. I could not see the mountain-peaks and did not know one direction from another. Even when Jim struck out of our trail and went off alone toward Holston I could not form an idea of where I was. All this, however, added to my feeling of the bigness of Penetier.

Dick was taciturn, and old Hiram, when I tried to engage him in conversation, cut me off with the remark that I would need my breath on the morrow. This somewhat offended me. So I made my bed and rolled into it. Not till I had lain quiet for a little did I realize that every bone and muscle felt utterly worn out. I seemed to

deaden and stiffen more each moment. Presently
Dick breathed heavily and Hiram snored. The
red glow of fire paled and died. I heard the clinking of the hobbles on Target, and a step, now
and then, of the other horses. The sky grew ever
bluer and colder, the stars brighter and larger,
and the night wind moaned in the pines. I heard
a coyote bark, a trout splash in the pool, and
the hoot of an owl. Then the sounds and the
clear, cold night seemed to fade away.

When Dick roused me the forest was shrouded
in gray, cold fog. No time was lost in getting
breakfast, driving in the horses, and packing.
Hardly any words were exchanged. My comrades appeared even soberer than on the day before. The fog lifted quickly that morning, and
soon the sun was shining.

We got under way at once, and took to the
trail at a jog-trot. I knew my horse better and
he was more used to me, which made it at least
bearable to both of us. Before long the cañon
widened out into the level forest land thickly
studded with magnificent pines. I had again the
feeling of awe and littleness. Everything was sol-
emn and still. The morning air was cool, and
dry as toast; the smell of pitch-pine choked my
nostrils. We rode briskly down the broad brown
aisles, across the sunny glades, under the mur-
muring pines.

The old hunter was leading our train, and evidently knew perfectly what he was about. Un-
expectedly he halted, bringing us up short. The

pack-ponies lined up behind us. Hiram looked at Dick.

"I smell smoke," he said, sniffing at the fragrant air.

Dick stared at the old hunter and likewise sniffed. I followed their lead, but all I could smell was the thick, piney odor of the forest.

"I don't catch it," replied Dick.

We continued on our journey perhaps for a quarter of a mile, and then Hiram Bent stopped again. This time he looked significantly at Dick without speaking a word.

"Ah!" exclaimed Dick. I thought his tone sounded queer, but it did not at the moment strike me forcibly. We rode on. The forest became lighter, glimpses of sky showed low down through the trees, we were nearing a slope.

For the third time the old hunter brought us to a stop, this time on the edge of a slope that led down to the rolling foot-hills. I could only stand and gaze. Those open stretches, sloping down, all green and brown and beautiful, robbed me of thought.

"Look thar!" cried Hiram Bent.

His tone startled me. I faced about, to see his powerful arm outstretched and his finger pointing. His stern face added to my sudden concern. Something was wrong with my friends. I glanced in the direction he indicated. There were two rolling slopes or steps below us, and they were like gigantic swells of a green ocean. Beyond the second one rose a long, billowy, bluish cloud. It

176

was smoke. All at once I smelled smoke, too. It came on the fresh, strong wind.

"Forest fire!" exclaimed Dick.

"Wal, I reckon," replied Hiram, tersely. "An' look thar, an' thar!"

Far to the right and far to the left, over the green, swelling foot-hills, rose that rounded, changing line of blue cloud.

"The slash! the slash! Buell's fired the slash!" cried Dick, as one suddenly awakened. "Penetier will go!"

"Wal, I reckon. But thet's not the worst."

"You mean —"

"Mebbe we can't get out. The forest's dry as powder, an' thet's the worst wind we could have. These cañon-draws suck in the wind, an' fire will race up them fast as a hoss can run."

"Good God, man! What'll we do?"

"Wait. Mebbe it ain't so bad — yet. Now let's all listen."

The faces of my friends, more than words, terrified me. I listened with all my ears while watching with all my eyes. The line of rolling cloud expanded, seemed to burst and roll upward, to bulge and mushroom. In a few short moments it covered the second slope as far to the right and left as we could see. The under surface was a bluish white. It shot up swiftly, to spread out into immense, slow-moving clouds of creamy yellow.

"Hear thet?" Hiram Bent shook his gray head as one who listened to dire tidings.

The wind, sweeping up the slope of Penetier, carried a strong, pungent odor of burning pitch. It brought also a low roar, not like the wind in the trees or rapid-rushing water. It might have been my imagination, but I fancied it was like the sound of flames blowing through the wood of a camp-fire.

"Fire! Fire!" exclaimed Hiram, with another ominous shake of his head. "We must be up an' doin'."

"The forest's greatest foe! Old Penetier is doomed!" cried Dick Leslie. "That line of fire is miles long, and is spreading fast. It'll shoot up the cañons and crisscross the forest in no time. Bent, what'll we do?"

"Mebbe we can get around the line. We must, or we'll have to make tracks for the mountain, an' thet's a long chance. You take to the left an' I'll go to the right, an' we'll see how the fire's runnin'."

"What will Ken do?"

"Wal, let him stay here — no, thet won't do! We might get driven back a little an' have to circle. The safest place in this forest is where we camped. Thet's not far. Let him drive the ponies back thar an' wait."

"All right. Ken, you hustle the pack-team back to our last night's camp. Wait there for us. We won't be long."

Dick galloped off through the forest, and Hiram went down the slope in almost the opposite direction. Left alone, I turned my horse and drove the pack-ponies along our back-trail. Thus engaged, I began to recover somewhat from the terror that had stupefied me. Still, I kept looking back. I found the mouth of the cañon and the trail, and in what I thought a very short time reached the bare, rocky spot where we had last camped. The horses all drank thirstily, and I discovered that I was hot and dry.

Then I waited. At every glance I expected to see Dick and Hiram riding up the cañon. But moments dragged by, and they did not come. Here there was no sign of smoke, nor even the faintest hint of the roar of the fire. The wind blew strongly up the cañon, and I kept turning my ear to it. In spite of the fact that my friends did not come quickly I had begun to calm my fears. They would return presently with knowledge of the course of the fire and the way to avoid it. My thoughts were mostly occupied with sorrow for beautiful Penetier. What a fiend Buell was! I had heard him say he would fire the slash, and he had kept his word.

Half an hour passed. I saw a flash of gray down the cañon, and shouted in joy. But what I thought Dick and Hiram was a herd of deer. They were running wildly. They clicked on the stones, and scarcely swerved for the pack-ponies. It took no second glance to see that they were fleeing from the fire. This brought back all my alarms, and every moment that I waited thereafter added to them. I watched the trail and under the trees for my friends, and I scanned the sky for signs of the blue-white clouds of smoke. But I saw neither.

"Dick told me to wait here; but how long shall I wait?" I muttered. "Something's happened to him. If only I could see what that fire is doing!"

The camping-place was low down between two slopes, one of which was high and had a rocky cliff standing bare in the sunlight. I conceived the idea of climbing to it. I could not sit quietly waiting any longer. So, mounting Target, I put him up the slope. It was not a steep climb, still it was long and took considerable time. Before I reached the gray cliff I looked down over the forest to see the rolling, smoky clouds. We climbed higher and still higher, till Target reached the cliff and could go no farther. Leaping off, I tied him securely and bent my efforts to getting around on top of the cliff. If I had known what a climb it was I should not have attempted it, but I could not back out with the summit looming over me. It ran up to a ragged crag. Hot, exhausted, and out of breath, I at last got there.

As I looked I shouted in surprise. It seemed that the whole of Penetier was under my feet. The green slope disappeared in murky clouds of smoke. There were great pillars and huge banks of yellow and long streaks of black, and here and there, underneath, moving splashes of red. The thing did not stay still one instant. It changed so that I could not tell what it did look like. There were life and movement in it, and something terribly sinister. I tried to calculate how far distant the fire was and how fast it was coming, but that, in my state of mind, I could not do. The whole sweep of forest below me was burning. I felt the strong breeze and smelled the burnt wood. Puffs of white smoke ran out ahead of the main clouds, and I saw three of them widely separated. What they meant puzzled me. But all of a sudden I saw in front of the nearest a flickering gleam of red. Then I knew those white streams of smoke rose where the fire was being sucked up the cañons. They leaped along with amazing speed. It was then that I realized that Dick and Hiram had been caught by one of these offshoots of the fire, and had been compelled to turn away to save their lives. Perhaps they would both be lost. For a moment I felt faint, but I fought it off. I had to think of myself. It was every one for himself, and perhaps there was many a man caught on Penetier with only a slender chance for life.

"Oh! oh!" I cried, suddenly. "Herky, Bud, and Bill tied helpless in that cabin! Dick forgot them. They'll be burned to death!"

As I stood there, trembling at the thought of Herky and his comrades bound hand and foot, the first roar of the forest fire reached my ears. It threatened, but it roused my courage. I jumped as if I had been shot, and clattered down that crag with wings guiding my long leaps. No crevice or jumble of loose stones or steep descent daunted me. I reached the horse, and, grasping the bridle, I started to lead him. We had zigzagged up, we went straight down. Target was too spirited to balk, but he did everything else. More than once he reared with his hoofs high in the air, and, snorting, crashed down. He pulled me off my feet, he pawed at me with his great iron shoes. When we got clear of the roughest and most thickly over-grown part of the descent I mounted him. Then I needed no longer to urge him. The fire had entered the cañon, the hollow roar swept up and filled Target with the same fright that possessed me. He plunged down, slid on his haunches, jumped the logs, crashed through brush. I had continually to rein him toward the camp. He wanted to turn from that hot wind and strange roar.

We reached a level, the open, stony ground, then the pool. The pack-ponies were standing patiently with drooping heads. The sun was obscured in thin blue haze. Smoke and dust and ashes blew by with the wind. I put Target's nose down to the water, so that he would drink. Then I cut packs off the ponies, spilled the contents, and filled my pockets with whatever I could lay my hands on in the way of eatables. I hung a canteen on the pommel, and threw a bag of biscuits over the saddle and tied it fast. My fingers worked swiftly. There was a fluttering in my throat, and my sight was dim. All the time the roar of the forest fire grew louder and more ominous.

The ponies would be safe. I would be safe in

the lee of the big rocks near the pool. But I did not mean to stay. I could not stay with those men lying tied up in the cabin. Herky had saved me. Still it was not that which spurred me on.

Target snorted shrilly and started back from the water, ready to stampede. Slipping the bridle into place, I snapped the bit between his teeth. I had to swing off my feet to pull his head down.

Even as I did this I felt the force of the wind. It was hard to breathe. A white tumbling column of smoke hid sky and sun. All about me it was like a blue twilight.

The appalling roar held me spellbound with my foot in the stirrup. It drew my glance even in that moment of flight.

Under the shifting cloud flashes of red followed by waves of fire raced through the tree-tops. That the forest fire travelled through the tree-tops was as new to me as it was terrible. The fire seemed to make and drive the wind. Lower down along the ground was a dull furnace-glow, now dark, now bright. It all brought into my mind a picture I had seen of the end of the world.

Target broke the spell by swinging me up into the saddle as he leaped forward with a furious snort. I struck him with the bridle, and yelled:

"You iron-jawed brute! You've been crazy to run — now run."

XVII

The Back-Fire

Target pounded over the scaly ground and thundered into the hard trail. Then he stretched out. As we cleared the last obstructing pile of rocks I looked back. There was a vast wave of fire rolling up the cañon and spreading up the slopes.

It was so close that I nearly fainted. With both hands knotted and stiff I clung to the pommel in a cold horror, and I looked back no more to see the flames reaching out for me. But I could not keep the dreadful roar from filling my ears, and it weakened me so that I all but dropped from the saddle. Only an unconscious instinct to fight for life made me hold on.

Blue and white puffs of smoke swept by me. The trail was a dim, twisting line. The slopes and pines, merged in a mass, flew backward in brown sheets. Above the roar of the pursuing fire I heard the thunder of Target's hoofs. I scarcely felt him or the saddle, only a motion and the splitting of the wind.

The fear of death by fire, which had almost robbed me of strength, passed from me. My brain cleared. Still I had no kind of hope, only a desperate resolve not to give up.

The great bay horse was running to save his life and to save mine. It was a race with fire. When I thought of the horse, and saw how fast he was going, and realized that I must do my part, I was myself again.

The trail was a winding, hard-packed thread of white ground. It had been made for leisurely travel. Many turns were sudden and sharp. I loosened the reins, and cried out to Target. Evidently I had unknowingly held him in, for he lengthened out, and went on in quicker, longer leaps. In that moment riding seemed easy. I listened to the roar behind me, now a little less deafening, and began to thrill. We were running away from the fire.

Hope made the race seem different. Something stirred and beat warm within me, driving out the chill in my marrow. I leaned over the neck of the great bay horse, and called to him and cheered him on. Then I saw he was deaf and blind to me, for he was wild. He had the bit between his teeth, and was running away.

The roar behind us relentlessly pursuing, only a little less appalling, was now not my only source of peril. Target could no more be guided nor stopped than could the forest fire. The trail grew more winding and overhung more thickly by pine branches. The horse did not swerve an inch for tree or thicket, but ran as if free, and the saving of my life began to be a matter of dodging. Once a crashing blow from a branch almost knocked me from the saddle. The wind in my ears half drowned the roar behind me. With hands twisted in Target's mane I bent low, watching with keen eyes for the trees and branches ahead. I drew up my knees and bent my body, and dodged and went down flat over the pommel like a wild-riding Indian. Target kept that straining run for a longer distance than I could judge. With the same break-neck speed he thundered on over logs and little washes, through the thick, bordering bushes, and around the sudden turns. His foam moistened my face and flecked my sleeves. The wind came stinging into my face, the heavy roar followed at my back with its menace.

Swift and terrible as the forest fire was, Target was winning the race. I knew it. Steadily the roar softened, but it did not die away. Pound! pound! pound! The big bay charged up the trail. How long could he stand that killing pace? I began to talk soothingly to him, to pull on the bridle; but he might have been an avalanche for all he heeded. Still I kept at him, fighting him every moment that I was free from low branches. Gradually the strain began to tell.

The sight of a cabin brought back to my mind the meaning of the wild race with fire. I had forgotten the prisoners. I had reached the forest glade and the cabin, but Target was still going hard. What if I could not stop him! Summoning all my strength, I quickly threw weight and muscle back on the reins and snapped the bit out of his teeth. Then coaxing, commanding, I pulled him back. In the glade were four horses, standing bunched with heads and ears up, uneasy, and beginning to be frightened. Perhaps the sight of them helped me to stop Target; at any rate, he slackened his pace and halted. He was spotted with foam, dripping wet, and his broad sides heaved.

I jumped off, stiff and cramped. I could scarcely walk. The air was clear, though the fog of smoke overspread the sun. The wind blew strong with a scent of pitch. Now that I was not riding, the roar of the fire sounded close. I caught the same strange growl, the note of onsweeping fury. Again the creepy cold went over me. I felt my face blanch, and the skin tighten over my cheeks. I dashed into the cabin, crying: "Fire! Fire! Fire!"

"Whoop! It's the kid!" yelled Herky-Jerky.

He was lying near the door, red as a brick in the face, and panting hard. In one cut I severed the rope on his feet; in another, that round his raw and bloody wrists. Herky had torn his flesh trying to release his hands.

"Kid, how'd you git back hyar?" he questioned, with his sharp little eyes glinting on me. "Did the fire chase you? Whar's Leslie?"

"Buell fired the slash. Penetier is burning. Dick and Hiram sent me back to the pool below, and then didn't come. They got — oh! . . . I'm afraid — lost! . . . Then I remembered you fellows. The fire's coming — it's awful — we must fly!"

"You thought of us?" Herkey's voice sounded queer and strangled. "Bud! Bill! Did you hear thet? Wal, wal!"

While he muttered on I cut Bill's bonds. He rose without a word. Bud was almost unconscious. He had struggled terribly. His heels had dug a hole in the hard clay floor; his wrists were skinned; his mouth and chin covered with earth, probably from his having bitten the ground in his agony. Herky helped him up and gave him a drink from a little pocket-flask.

"Herky, if you think you've rid some in your day, look at thet hoss," said Bill, coolly, from the door. He eyed me coolly; in fact, he was as cool as if there were no fire on Penetier. But Bud was white and sick, and Herky flaming with excitement.

"We hain't got a chance. Listen! Thet roar! She's hummin'."

"It's runnin' up the draw. We don't stand no show down in hyar. Grab a hoss now, an' we'll try to head across the ridge."

I remounted Target, and the three men caught horses and climbed up bareback. Bill led the way across the glade, up the slope, into the level forest. There we broke into a gallop. The air upon this higher ground was dark and thick, but not so hard to breathe as that lower down. We pressed on. For a while the roar receded, and almost deadened. Then it grew clearer again, filled out, and swelled. Bud wanted to sheer off to the left. Herky swore we were being surrounded. Bill turned a deaf ear to them. From my own sense of direction I fancied we were going wrong, but Bill was so cool he gave me courage. Soon a blue, windy haze, shrouding the giant pines ahead, caused Bill to change his course.

"Do you know whar you're headin'!" yelled Herky, high above the roar.

"I hadn't got the least idee, Herky," shouted Bill, as cool as could be, "but I guess somewhar whar it'll be hot!"

We were lost in the forest and almost surrounded by fire, if the roar was anything to tell by. We galloped on, always governed by the roar, always avoiding the slope up the mountain. If we once started up that with the fire in our rear we were doomed. Perhaps there were times when the wind deceived us. It was hard to tell. Anyway, we kept on, growing more bewildered. Bud looked like a dead man already and reeled in his saddle. The horses were getting hard to manage, and the wind was strengthening and puffed at us from all quarters. Bill still looked cool, but the last vestige of color had faded from his face. These things boded ill. Herky had grown strangely silent, which fact was the worst of all for me. For that tough, scarred, reckless little wretch to hold his tongue was the last straw.

The air freshened somewhat, and the forest lightened. Almost abruptly we rode out to the edge of a great, wide cañon. It must have crossed the forest at right angles to the cañon we had left. It was twice as wide and deep as any I had yet seen. In the bottom wound a broad brook.

"Which way now?" asked Herky.

Bill shook his head. Far to our right a pall of smoke moved over the tree-tops, to our left was foggy gloom, behind rolled the unceasing roar. We all looked straight across. Probably each of us harbored the same thought. Before that wind the fire would leap the cañon in flaming bounds, and on the opposite level was the thick pitch-pine forest of Penetier proper. So far we had been among the foot-hills. We dared not enter the real forest with that wild-fire back of us. Momentarily we stood irresolute. It was a pause full of hopelessness, such as might have come to tired deer, close-harried by hounds.

The winding brook and the brown slope, comparatively bare of trees, brought me a sudden inspiration.

"Back-fire! Back-fire!" I cried to my companions, in wild appeal. "We must back-fire! It's our chance! Here's the place!"

Bud scowled and Herky grumbled, but Bill grasped at the idea.

"I've heerd of back-firin'. The rangers do it. But how? How?"

They caught his hope, and their haggard faces lightened.

"Kid, we ain't forest rangers," said Herky. "Do you know what you're talkin' about?"

"Yes, yes! Come on! We'll back-fire!"

I led the way down the slope, and they came close at my heels. I rode into the shallow brook, and dismounted about the middle between the banks. I hung my coat on the pommel of my saddle.

"Bud, you and Bill hold the horses here!" I shouted, intensely excited. "Herky, have you matches?"

"Nary a match."

"Hyar's a box," said Bill, tossing it.

"Come on, Herky! You run up the brook. Light a match, and drop it every hundred feet. Be sure it catches. Lucky there's little wind down here. Go as far as you can. I'll run down!"

We splashed out of the brook and leaped up the bank. The grass was long and dry. There was brush near by, and the pine-needle mats almost bordered the bank. I struck a match and dropped it.

Sis-s-s! Flare! It was almost like dropping a spark into gunpowder. The flame ran quickly, reached the pine-needles, then sputtered and fizzed into a big blaze. The first pine-tree exploded and went off like a rocket. We were startled by the sound and the red, up-leaping pillar of fire. Sudden heat shot back at us as if from a furnace. Great sparks began to fall.

"It's goin'!" yelled Herky-Jerky, his voice ringing strong. He clapped his hat down on my bare head. Then he started running up-stream.

I darted in the opposite direction. I heard Bud

and Bill yelling, and the angry crack and hiss of the fire. A few rods down I stopped, struck another match, and lit the grass. There was a sputter and flash. Then the flame flared up, spread like running quicksilver, and, meeting the pine-needles, changed to red. I ran on. There was a loud flutter behind me, then a crack almost like a shot, then a seething roar. Another pine had gone off. As I stopped to strike the third match there came three distinct reports, and then others that seemed dulled in a windy roar. I raced onward, daring only once to look back. A fearful sight met my gaze. The slope was a red wave. The pines were tufts of flame. The air was filled with steaming clouds of whirling smoke. Then I fled onward again.

Match after match I struck, and when the box was empty I must have been a mile, two miles, maybe more, from the starting-point. I was wringing-wet, and there was a piercing pain in my side. I plunged across the brook, and in as deep water as I could find knelt down to cover all but my face. Then, with laboring breaths that bubbled the water near my mouth, I kept still and watched.

The back-fire which I had started swept up over the slope and down the brook like a charge of red lancers. Spears of flame led the advance. The flame licked up the dry surface-grass and brush, and, meeting the pines, circled them in a whirlwind of fire, like lightning flashing upward. Then came prolonged reports, and after that a long, blistering roar in the tree-tops. Even as I gazed, appalled in the certainty of a horrible fate, I thrilled at the grand spectacle. Fire had always fascinated me. The clang of the engines and the call of "Fire!" would tear me from any task or play. But I had never known what fire was. I knew now. Storms of air and sea were nothing compared to this. It was the greatest force in nature. It was fire. On one hand, I seemed cool and calculated the chances; on the other, I had flashes in my brain, and kept crying out crazily, in a voice like a whisper: "Fire! Fire! Fire!"

But presently the wall of fire rolled by and took the roar with it. Dense billows of smoke followed, and hid everything in opaque darkness. I heard the hiss of falling sparks and the crackle of burning wood, and occasionally the crash of a falling branch. It was intolerably hot, but I could stand the heat better than the air. I coughed and strangled. I could not get my breath. My eyes smarted and burned. Crawling close under the bank, I leaned against it and waited.

Some hours must have passed. I suffered, not exactly pain, but a discomfort that was almost worse. By-and-by the air cleared a little. Rifts in the smoke drifted over me, always toward the far side of the cañon. Twice I crawled out upon the bank, but the heat drove me back into the water. The snow-water from the mountain-peaks had changed from cold to warm; still, it gave a relief from the hot blast of air. More time dragged by. Weary to the point of collapse, I grew not to care about anything.

Then the yellow fog lightened, and blew across the brook and lifted and split. The parts of the cañon-slope that I could see were seared and blackened. The pines were columns of living coals. The fire was eating into their hearts. Presently they would snap at the trunk, crash down, and burn to ashes. Wreathes of murky smoke circled them, and drifted aloft to join the overhanging clouds.

I floundered out on the bank, and began to walk up-stream. After all, it was not so very hot, but I felt queer. I did not seem to be able to step where I looked or see where I stepped. Still, that caused me no worry. The main thing was that the fire had not yet crossed the brook. I wanted to feel overjoyed at that, but I was too tired. Anyway I was sure the fire had crossed below or above. It would be tearing down on this side presently, and then I would have to crawl into the brook or burn up. It did not matter much which I had to do. Then I grew dizzy, my legs trembled, my feet lost all sense of touching the ground. I could not go much farther.

Just then I heard a shout. It was close by. I answered, and heard heavy steps. I peered through the smoky haze. Something dark moved up in the gloom.

"Ho, kid! Thar you are!" . . . I felt a strong arm go round my waist. "Wal, wal!" That was

Herky. His voice sounded glad. It roused a strange eagerness in me; his rough greeting seemed to bring me back from a distance.

"All wet, but not burned none, I see. We kinder was afeared. . . . Say, kid, thet back-fire, now. It was a dandy. It did the biz. Our whiskers was singed, but we're safe. An, kid, it was your game, played like a man."

After that his voice grew faint, and I felt as if I were walking in a dream.

XVIII

Conclusion

That dreadful feeling of motion went away, and I became unconscious of everything. When I awoke the sun was gleaming dimly through thin films of smoke. I was lying in a pleasant little ravine with stunted pines fringing its slopes. The brook bowled merrily over stones.

Bud snored in the shade of a big bowlder. Herky whistled as he broke dead branches into fagots for a camp-fire. Bill was nowhere in sight. I saw several of the horses browsing along the edge of the water.

My drowsy eyelids fell back again. When I awoke a long time seemed to have passed. The air was clearer, the sky darker, and the sun had gone behind the peaks. I saw Bill and Herky skinning a deer.

"Where are we?" I asked, sitting up.

"Hello, kid!" replied Herky, cheerily. "We come up to the head of the cañon, thet's all. How're you feelin'?"

"I'm all right, only tired. Where's the forest fire?"

"It's most burned out by now. It didn't jump the cañon into the big forest. Thet back-fire did the biz. Say, kid, wasn't settin' off them pines an' runnin' fer your life jest like bein' in a battle?"

"It certainly was. Herky, how long will we be penned up here?"

"Only a day or two. I reckon we'd better not risk takin' you back to Holston till we're sure about the fire. Anyways, kid, you need rest. You're all played out."

Indeed, I was so weary that it took an effort to lift my hand. A strange lassitude made me indifferent. But Herky's calm mention of taking me back to Holston changed the color of my mood. I began to feel more cheerful. The meal we ate was scant enough   biscuits and steaks of broiled venison with a pinch of salt; but, starved as we were, it was more than satisfactory. Herky and Bill were absurdly eager to serve me. Even Bud was kind to me, though he still wore conspicuously over his forehead the big bruise I had given him. After I had eaten I began to gain strength. But my face was puffed from the heat, my injured arm was stiff and sore, and my legs seemed never to have been used before.

Darkness came on quickly. The dew fell heavily, and the air grew chilly. Our blazing camp-fire was a comfort. Bud and Bill carried in logs for firewood, while Herky made me a bed of dry pine-needles.

"It'll be some cold to-night," he said, "an' we'll hev to hug the fire. Now if we was down in the foot-hills we'd be warmer, hey? Look thar!"

He pointed down the ravine, and I saw a great white arc of light extending up into the steely sky.

"The forest fire?"

"Yep, she's burnin' some. But you oughter seen it last night. Not thet it ain't worth seein' jest now. Come along with me."

He led me where the ravine opened wide. I felt, rather than saw, a steep slope beneath. Far down was a great patch of fire. It was like a crazy quilt, here dark, there light, with streaks and stars and streams of fire shining out of the blackness. Masses of slow-moving smoke overhung the brighter areas. The night robbed the forest fire of its fierceness and lent it a kind of glory. The fire had ceased to move; it had spent its force, run its race, and was now dying. But I could not forget what it had been, what it had done. Thousands of acres of magnificent pines had perished. The shade and color and beauty of that part of the forest had gone. The heart of the great trees was now slowly rolling away in those dark, weird clouds of smoke. I was sad for the loss and sick with fear for Dick and Hiram.

Herky must have known my mind.

"You needn't feel bad, kid. Thet's only a foothill or so of Penetier gone up in smoke. An' Buell's sawmill went, too. It's almost a sure thing thet Leslie an' old Bent got out safe, though they must be doin' some tall worryin' about you. I wonder how they feel about me an'

Bud an' Bill? A little prematoore roastin' for us, eh? Wal, wal!"

We went back to the camp. I lay down near the fire and fell asleep. Some time in the night I awoke. The fire was still burning brightly. Bud and Bill were lying with their backs to it almost close enough to scorch. Herky sat in his shirt-sleeves. The smoke of his pipe and the smoke of the camp-fire wafted up together. Then I saw and felt that he had covered me with his coat and vest.

I slept far into the next day. Herky was in camp alone. The others had gone, Herky said, and he would not tell me where. He did not appear as cheerful as usual. I suspected he had quarrelled with his companions, very likely about what was to be done with me. The day passed, and again I slept. Herky awakened me before it was light.

"Come, kid, we'll rustle in to Holston to-day."

We cooked our breakfast of venison, and then Herky went in search of the horses. They had browsed far up the ravine, and the dawn had broken by the time he returned. Target stood well to be saddled, nor did he bolt when I climbed up. Perhaps that ride I gave him had chastened and subdued his spirit. Well, it had nearly killed me. Herky mounted the one horse left, a sorry-looking pack-pony, and we started down the ravine.

An hour of steady descent passed by before we caught sight of any burned forest land. Then as we descended into the big cañon we turned a curve and saw, far ahead to the left, a black, smoky, hideous slope. We kept to the right side of the brook and sheered off just as we reached a point opposite, where the burned line began. Fire had run up that side till checked by bare weathered slopes and cliffs. As far down the brook as eye could see through the smoky haze there stretched that black line of charred, spear-pointed pines, some glowing, some blazing, all smoking.

From time to time, as we climbed up the slope, I looked back. The higher I got the more hideous became the outlook over the burned district. I was glad when Herky led the way into the deep shade of level forest, shutting out the view. It would take a hundred years to reforest those acres denuded of their timber by the fire of a few days.

But as hour after hour went by, with our trail leading through miles and miles of the same old forest that had bewitched me, I began to feel a little less grief at the thought of what the fire had destroyed. It was a loss, yet only a small part of vast Penetier. If only my friends had gotten out alive!

Herky was as relentless in his travelling as I had found him in some other ways. He kept his pony at a trot. The trail was open, we made fast time, and when the sun had begun to cast a shadow before us we were going down-hill. Busy with the thought of my friends, I scarcely noted the passing of time. It was a surprise to me when we rode down the last little foot-hill, out into the scattered pines, and saw Holston only a few miles across the sage-flat.

"Wal, kid, we've come to the partin' of the ways," said Herky, with a strange smile on his smug face.

"Herky, won't you ride in with me?"

"Naw, I reckon it'd not be healthy fer me."

"But you haven't even a saddle or blanket or any grub."

"I've a friend across hyar a ways, a rancher, an' he'll fix me up. But, kid, I'd like to hev thet hoss. He was Buell's, an' Buell owed me money. Now I calkilate you can't take Target back East with you, an' you might as well let me have him."

"Sure, Herky." I jumped off at once, led the horse over, and held out the bridle. Herky dismounted, and began fumbling with the stirrup straps.

"Your legs are longer'n mine," he explained.

"Oh yes, Herky, I almost forgot to return your hat," I said, removing the wide sombrero. It had a wonderful band made of horsehair and a buckle of silver with a strange device.

"Wal, you keep the hat," he replied, with his back turned. "Greaser stole your hoss an' your outfit's lost, an' you might want somethin' to remember your — your friends in Arizony. . . . Thet hat ain't much, but, say, the buckle was an Injun's I shot, an' I made the band when I was in jail in Yuma."

"Thank you, Herky. I'll keep it, though I'd never need anything to make me remember Arizona — or you."

Herky swung his bow-legs over Target and I got astride the lean-backed pony. There did not seem to be any more to say, yet we both lingered.

"Good-bye, Herky, I'm glad I met you," I said, offering my hand.

He gave it a squeeze that nearly crushed my fingers. His keen little eyes gleamed, but he turned away without another word, and, slapping Target on the flank, rode off under the trees.

I put the hat back on my head and watched Herky for a moment. His silence and abrupt manner were unlike him, but what struck me most was the fact that in our last talk every word had been clean and sincere. Somehow it pleased me. Then I started the pony toward Holston.

He was tired and I was ready to drop, and those last few miles were long. We reached the out-skirts of the town perhaps a couple of hours before sundown. A bank of clouds had spread out of the west and threatened rain.

The first person I met was Cless, and he put the pony in his corral and hurried me round to the hotel. On the way he talked so fast and said so much that I was bewildered before we got there. The office was full of men, and Cless shouted to them. There was the sound of a chair scraping hard on the floor, then I felt myself clasped by brawny arms. After that all was rather hazy in my mind. I saw Dick and Jim and old Hiram, though I could not see them distinctly, and I heard them all talking, all questioning at once. Then I was talking in a somewhat silly way, I thought, and after that some one gave me a hot, nasty drink, and I felt the cool sheets of a bed.

The next morning all was clear. Dick came to my room and tried to keep me in bed, but I refused to stay. We went down to breakfast, and sat at a table with Jim and Hiram. It seemed to me that I could not answer any questions till I had asked a thousand.

What news had they for me? Buell had escaped, after firing the slash. His sawmill and lumber-ramp and fifty thousand acres of timber had been burned. The fire had in some way been confined to the foot-hills. It had rained all night, so the danger of spreading was now over. My letter had brought the officers of the forest service; even the Chief, who had been travelling west over the Santa Fé, had stopped off and was in Holston then. There had been no arrests, nor would there be, unless Buell or Stockton could be found. A new sawmill was to be built by the service. Buell's lumbermen would have employment in the mill and as rangers in the forest.

But I was more interested in matters which Dick seemed to wish to avoid.

"How did you get out of the burning forest?" I asked, for the second time.

"We didn't get out. We went back to the pool

where we sent you. The pack-ponies were there, but you were gone. By George! I was mad, and then I was just broken up. I was afraid you'd been burned. We weathered the fire all right, and then rode in to Holston. Now the mystery is — where were you?"

"Then you saved all the ponies?"

"Yes, and brought your outfit in. But, Ken, we — that was awful of us to forget those poor fellows tied fast in the cabin." Dick looked haggard, there was a dark gloom in his eyes, and he gulped. Then I knew why he avoided certain references to the fire. "To be burned alive . . . horrible! I'll never get over it. It'll haunt me always. Of course we had to save our own lives; we had no time to go to them. Yet —"

"Don't let it worry you, Dick," I interrupted.

"What do you mean?" he asked, slowly.

"Why, I beat the fire up to the cabin, that's all. Buell's horse can run some. I cut the men loose, and we made up across the ridge, got lost, surrounded by fire, and then I got Herky to help me start a back-fire in that big cañon."

"Back-fire!" exclaimed Dick, slamming the table with his big fist. Then he settled down and looked at me. Hiram looked at me. Jim looked at me, and not one of them said a word for what seemed a long time. It brought the blood to my face. But for all my embarrassment it was sweet praise. At last Dick broke the silence.

"Ken Ward, this stumps me! . . . Tell us about it."

So I related my adventures from the moment they had left me till we met again.

"It was a wild boy's trick, Ken — that ride in the very face of fire in a dry forest. But, thank God, you saved the lives of those fellows!"

"Amen!" exclaimed old Hiram, fervently. "My lad, you saved Penetier, too; thar's no doubt on it. The fire was sweepin' up the cañon, an' it would have crossed the brook somewhars in thet stretch you back-fired."

"Ken, yu shore was born in Texas," drawled Jim Williams.

His remark was unrelated to our talk, I did not know what he meant by it; nevertheless it pleased me more than anything that had ever been said to me in my life.

Then came the reading of letters that had arrived for me. In Hal's letter, first and last he harped on having been left behind. Father sent me a check, and wrote that in the event of any trouble in the lumber district he trusted me to take the first train for Harrisburg. That, I knew, meant that I must get out of my ragged clothes. This I did, and packed them up — all except Herky's sombrero, which I wore. Then I went to the railroad station to see the schedule, and I compromised with father by deciding to take the limited. The fast east-bound train had gone a little before, and the next one did not leave until six o'clock. This would give me half a day with my friends.

When I returned to the hotel Dick was looking

for me. He carried me off up-stairs to a hall full of men. At one end were tables littered with papers, and here men were signing their names. Dick explained that forest rangers were being paid and new ones hired. Then he introduced me to officers of the service and the Chief. I knew by the way they looked at me that Dick had been talking. It made me so tongue-tied that I could not find my voice when the Chief spoke to me and shook my hand warmly. He was a tall man, with a fine face and kind eyes and hair just touched with gray.

"Kenneth Ward," he went on, pleasantly, "I hope that letter of introduction I dictated for you some time ago has been of some service."

"I haven't had a chance to use it yet," I blurted out, and I dived into my pocket to bring forth the letter. It was wrinkled, soiled, and had been soaked with water. I began to apologize for its disreputable appearance when he interrupted me.

"I've heard about the ducking you got and all the rest of it," he said, smiling. Then his manner changed to one of business and hurry.

"You are studying forestry?"

"Yes, sir. I'm going to college this fall."

"My friend in Harrisburg wrote me of your ambition and, I may say, aptness for the forest service. I'm very much pleased. We need a host of bright young fellows. Here, look at this map."

He drew my attention to a map lying on the table, and made crosses and tracings with a pencil while he talked.

"This is Penetier. Here are the Arizona Peaks. The heavy shading represents timbered land. All these are cañons. Here's Oak Creek Cañon, the one the fire bordered. Now I want you to tell me how you worked that back-fire, and, if you can, mark the line you fired."

This appeared to me an easy task, and certainly one I was enthusiastic over. I told him just how I had come to the cañon, and how I saw that the fire would surely cross there, and that a back-fire was the only chance. Then, carefully studying the map, I marked off the three miles Herky and I had fired.

"Very good. You had help in this?"

"Yes. A fellow called Herky-Jerky. He was one of Buell's men who kept me a prisoner."

"But he turned out a pretty good sort, didn't he?"

"Indeed, yes, sir."

"Well, I'll try to locate him and offer him a job in the service. Now, Mr. Ward, you've had special opportunities; you have an eye in your head, and you are interested in forestry. Perhaps you can help us. Personally I shall be most pleased to hear what you think might be done in Penetier."

I gasped and stared, and could scarcely believe my ears. But he was not joking; he was as serious as if he had addressed himself to one of his officers. I looked at them all, standing interested and expectant. Dick was as grave and erect as a deacon. Jim seemed much impressed. But old

Hiram Bent, standing somewhat back of the others, deliberately winked at me.

But for that wink I never could have seized my opportunity. It made me remember my talks with Hiram. So I boiled down all that I had learned and launched it on the Chief. Whether I was brief or not, I was out of breath when I stopped. He appeared much surprised.

"Thank you," he said, finally. "You certainly have been observant." Then he turned to his officers. "Gentlemen, here's a new point of view from first-hand observation. I call it splendid conservation. It's in the line of my policy. It considers the settler and lumberman instead of combating him."

He shook hands with me again. "You may be sure I'll not lose sight of you. Of course you will be coming West next summer, after your term at college?"

"Yes, sir, I want to — if Dick —"

He smiled as I hesitated. That man read my mind like an open book.

"Mr. Leslie goes to the Coconina Forest as head forest ranger. Mr. Williams goes as his assistant. And I have appointed Mr. Bent game warden in the same forest. You may spend next summer with them."

I stammered some kind of thanks, and found myself going out and down-stairs with my friends.

"Oh, Dick! Wasn't he fine? . . . Say, where's Coconina Forest?"

"It's over across the desert and beyond the Grand Cañon of Arizona. Penetier is tame compared to Coconina. I'm afraid to let you come out there."

"I don't have to ask you, Mr. Dick," I replied.

"Lad, I'll need a young feller bad next summer," said old Hiram, with twinkling eyes. "One as can handle a rope, an' help tie up lions an' sich."

"Oh! my bear cub! I'd forgotten him. I wanted to take him home."

"Wal, thar weren't no sense in thet, youngster, fer you couldn't do it. He was a husky cub."

"I hate to give up my mustang, too. Dick, have you heard of the Greaser?"

"Not yet, but he'll be trailing into Holston before long."

Jim Williams removed his pipe, and puffed a cloud of white smoke.

"Ken, I shore ain't forgot Greaser," he drawled. with his slow smile. "Hev yu any pertickler thing yu want did to him?"

"Jim, don't kill him!" I burst out, impetuously, and then paused, frightened out of speech. Why I was afraid of him I did not know, he seemed so easy-going, so careless — almost sweet, like a woman; but then I had seen his face once with a look that I could never forget.

"Wal, Ken, I'll dodge Greaser if he ever crosses my trail again."

That promise was a relief. I knew Greaser would come to a bad end, and certainly would get his just deserts; but I did not want him punished any more for what he had done to me.

Those last few hours sped like winged moments. We talked and planned a little, I divided my outfit among my friends, and then it was time for the train. That limited train had been late, so they said, every day for a week, and this day it was on time to the minute. I had no luck.

My friends bade me good-bye as if they expected to see me next day, and I said good-bye calmly. I had my part to play. My short stay with them had made me somehow different. But my coolness was deceitful. Dick helped me on the train and wrung my hand again.

"Good-bye, Ken. It's been great to have you out. . . . Next year you'll be back in the forests!"

He had to hurry to get off. The train started as I looked out of my window. There stood the powerful hunter, his white head bare, and he was waving his hat. Jim leaned against a railing with his sleepy, careless smile. I caught a gleam of the blue gun swinging at his hip. Dick's eyes shone warm and blue; he was shouting something. Then they all passed back out of sight. So my gaze wandered to the indistinct black line of Penetier, to the purple slopes, and up to the cold, white mountain-peaks, and Dick's voice rang in my ears like a prophecy: "You'll be back in the forests!"

We hope you have enjoyed this Large Print book. Other G.K. Hall & Co. or Chivers Press Large Print books are available at your library or directly from the publishers.

For more information about current and upcoming titles, please call or write, without obligation, to:

G.K. Hall & Co.
P.O. Box 159
Thorndike, Maine 04986 USA
Tel. (800) 257-5157

OR

Chivers Press Limited
Windsor Bridge Road
Bath BA2 3AX
England
Tel. (0225) 335336

All our Large Print titles are designed for easy reading, and all our books are made to last.